The Sweetest Mistake

An O'Brien Brothers Novel

Susan Coventry

ISBN-13: 978-1721677559

ISBN-10: 1721677550

Cover Design: Woodchuck Arts
Edited by: FirstEditing.com

ALSO BY SUSAN COVENTRY

Chapter 1

Julia loved babies. She loved everything about them—their sweet little faces, tiny fingers and toes, soft skin, and toothless grins. In fact, she wouldn't mind having a house full of kids someday or at the very least two. But for now, she'd have to be satisfied interacting with babies at her father's pediatric practice, or so she thought.

As she stood on Connor's front porch, she swore she heard a baby crying inside. But it couldn't have been. Connor had just returned from a short trip to Denver, and Julia had come over to surprise him. He must have had company, but there weren't any cars parked in his driveway except for his Jeep Wrangler. Strange.

She hesitated to ring the doorbell but decided she was being silly. He'd been gone for three days, and she'd missed him even though he'd left under mysterious circumstances. He'd been cagey about the trip, telling her he just needed to get away for a few days and clear his head. Clear his head of what, she'd wondered, and why Denver? When she'd asked him, he'd said that he wanted to be in the mountains, and knowing his propensity for privacy, she'd tried not to question it too much.

Connor was the middle of three brothers who co-owned a successful landscaping design business in Brandon, a mostly rural community in southeast Michigan. Julia had met him through her best friend, Harper Davies, who was currently dating Connor's older brother, Finn.

At first, Julia hadn't wanted anything to do with the flirtatious, enigmatic O'Brien brother, but he'd slowly worn down her defenses, and now they'd been dating for almost five months. After a rocky start, their relationship had been starting to smooth out when Connor had suddenly taken off to Denver, leaving her to wonder what secret he was keeping this time.

Connor was good at keeping secrets, as she'd discovered early on. At first, he hadn't wanted to tell anyone they were dating, not even his brothers, and it had driven her crazy. She couldn't understand why he'd been so guarded, especially with the people he loved. She'd felt relieved when he'd finally agreed to share the news with their families and friends, only to encounter another obstacle.

When she'd taken him to meet her parents, they'd had a less-than-enthusiastic reaction. Especially her father, who'd had his heart set on her marrying his protégé, Alec, whom she'd dated prior to Connor. To her father, Dr. James Lee, a landscaper was nowhere near good enough for his only daughter. Her mom, Debra, had been less obvious, but Julia had sensed her disappointment too. It hadn't seemed to matter that Connor was a successful business owner. In their minds, she was supposed to have married Alec, and that was that.

So far, nothing about dating Connor had been easy, and they were different in so many ways that it was a miracle they were still together. Yet she was drawn to him in ways she didn't fully understand. Some might have called it chemistry, something she hadn't experienced with Alec but felt in spades with Connor. Others might have labeled it a physical attraction, and that's what it had been at first. She smiled as she remembered one of their early encounters...

Connor hopped out of his work truck and swaggered toward Capture the Moment Studio, where Julia worked with her best friend, Harper. She tried to ignore the outline of his sleek, toned body in his tight black T-shirt and ripped blue jeans. Tried not to wonder about the tattoo that peeked out from the right sleeve of his T-shirt. Instead, she returned her attention to the stack of invoices she'd been reviewing and acted like she hadn't seen him coming.

And then the studio door creaked open, and he came in and stood right next to her, casually leaning his hip against her desk. But still, she had enough willpower not to look up right away, even when she heard his deep, gravelly voice say, "Mornin', beautiful."

Next came the seriously difficult part. Connor had propped up his aviators in his cropped dark-brown hair and looked down at her through his dazzling slate-blue eyes with the laugh lines at the corners. On women, those lines would have been called wrinkles, but on Connor, they just added to his sex appeal. Not that she'd stared at them for long, because gazing into Connor's eyes was like looking directly at the sun— dangerous and potentially life-threatening.

"Harper's not here," Julia said.

"I didn't stop by to see Harper."

"Oh? Well then, you might as well get to work because, as you can, see I'm busy."

"Hmmm. Can I ask you a question?"

Realizing that she wasn't getting rid of him that easily, she set down her pen and sighed. "What is it?"

"Why don't you like me?"

Julia's eyes widened at the unexpected question, but the answer was simple. "Because you're too cocky."

Crossing his muscular arms over his equally muscular chest, he smiled. Smiled! See, cocky—just like she'd said.

"Some might call it confident."

"Some might, but in your case, it's cockiness."

"Didn't your mother ever teach you that when someone pretends *not* to like you, it's because, deep down, they actually do?"

"Didn't your mother ever teach *you* that it's not polite to look at women like they're a piece of chocolate?"

And then he laughed, his smile spreading out to encompass his gorgeous face. *Damn it.*

"What's wrong with telling a woman she's beautiful?"

"Nothing as long as you really mean it and you're not just saying it to try and get the woman to sleep with you."

"Is that what you think I'm doing?"

"Aren't you?"

Connor shook his head, that amused gleam still in his eyes. "I never said anything about sleeping together. That's all you, sweetheart."

"See! Right there," she said, stabbing the air with her index finger.

"Right where? What are you talking about?"

"There's an example of you being cocky. You think that all women want to sleep with you."

He laughed again. "You got something against sex?"

"What? NO!" She was becoming more exasperated by the moment. Why did this man have the power to make her so crazy?

"Well, despite what you think of me, I'm not after you for sex."

Julia narrowed her eyes at him. "You're not?"

"No. If that's what I wanted, all I'd have to do…well, never mind. The point is, I'd just like to get to know you better. Take you out to dinner or something. But it's obvious that you're not interested, so I'll just be on my way."

With that, Connor flipped down his aviators and started walking toward the door. She wasn't sure what possessed her, but she jumped up and shouted, "Wait!"

Placing his hands on his narrow hips, he tilted his head and said, "Yes?"

"Maybe I have been a little tough on you."
Okay, who possessed my body, and why is she doing this?

"Are you apologizing?"

"I don't know. Maybe."

Cocking an eyebrow at her, he said, "What *are* you doing, then?"

Good question. And then she blurted out, "Maybe we could go out for a drink sometime. You know, to get to know each other like you said."

If Connor's smile had been blinding before, now it was downright lethal. "A drink? With me? Are you sure you want to do that?"

"Don't press your luck. A simple yes or no will do."

Flipping his glasses back up again, he stared at her with those mesmerizing eyes and answered, "Hell yes." And then he turned and sauntered out the door.

It wasn't until she finally got her wits together that she realized they hadn't set a date. Instead of feeling relieved, she felt disgruntled. *Now what? Is he going to call me? Do I have to call him because it was my idea? Ugh! Why did I have to open my big fat mouth?*

The sound of a baby crying jolted her back to the present. This time, there was no mistaking it, and Julia's curiosity prompted her to ring the doorbell. She waited a minute, and when nobody answered, she rang it again, holding her finger down on the button and listening closely to make sure she heard it ring. And then she heard footsteps. *Finally.*

Instead of swinging open the door, Connor barely cracked it and poked his head out.

"Julia?" he said, looking surprised to see her there.

"Hi."

"Hi," he replied through the crack.

"Aren't you going to let me in?"

"It's not really a good time. Can I call you later?"

But before she could answer, she heard a baby cry even louder that time. "Are you *babysitting*?"

He sighed. "Not exactly."

"Connor? Who's there?" came an unfamiliar woman's voice.

Julia stilled, the blood rushing to her feet. *A woman and a baby?*

"Connor? What's going on?" Julia demanded.

"I'd like to know that too," the woman said from behind him.

Realizing that he was trapped, Connor swung open the door to reveal the woman behind the voice. And if Julia hadn't already been suspicious, she became even more so when she saw a beautiful blonde-haired woman holding a baby and looking completely at ease in Connor's house.

"You might as well come in," Connor muttered, stepping aside to let Julia through.

At that moment, she wasn't sure she wanted to. *Maybe she's a cousin or a distant relative.* Studying the woman closely, Julia searched for some resemblance to Connor.

"Connor? Aren't you going to introduce us?" the woman asked, looking Julia over as well.

But before he could make the introductions, the woman repositioned her baby so it was facing outward, and the resemblance Julia had been looking for was right there—in the baby's face. *Ohmigod, ohmigod. It can't be.*

In the next second, her fears were confirmed. Clearing his throat nervously, Connor said, "Uh…Julia. This is Camilla Robertson and her…*our*…daughter, Ava."

Suddenly, the room was spinning, and Julia reached out to grab onto something, fearing she would faint. Connor rushed forward and gripped her elbow tightly. "You okay?"

7

"Okay? Seriously?" *Wait a minute. Did I just say that aloud?*

Camilla wore a smug expression when she said, "So, I see you haven't told her yet."

Scowling, he said, "I just found out myself."

"How long *have* you known?" Julia asked, twisting out of Connor's grip. Her voice had risen along with her blood pressure, but she couldn't help it. She'd come here to surprise him, and instead, she'd been knocked flat. *Is it true? Is he really this baby's father?*

Looking between the two women, Connor said, "Let's sit down where we can talk."

Julia thought about turning around and bolting out the door, but Connor placed his hand on her elbow again and almost forcefully guided her into the living room.

Camilla was the only one who looked unaffected, and suddenly, Julia despised her even more then when she'd first learned about Cam. Over a year ago, Connor had caught Cam cheating on him with her boss, which was why he'd broken up with her. And now here she was, waltzing back into his life with his baby in tow.

Julia sat down on the couch, grateful to get off her shaky legs. Connor sat down beside her, but he left some distance between them, as if he were afraid she might haul off and smack him at any moment (which was extremely tempting).

Cam perched on a chair opposite them and bounced Ava on her knee. Julia was bursting with questions, but they were all stuck in her throat. All she could do was stare at the beautiful baby in Cam's arms and allow the reality to sink in. Connor was this child's father, and according to him, he'd just recently found out. If Julia was reeling, how must he be feeling? She vacillated between being pissed at him for not telling her sooner and feeling sorry for him. And then she glared at Cam, wondering why the woman had kept Ava a secret.

"In all fairness, I just sprang this on him a few weeks ago," Cam said evenly.

"How can you be sure—" Julia started to say.

"That Ava's his? Can't you tell by looking at her?" Cam said.

Julia had seen the resemblance right away, but what about Cam's boss? Couldn't Ava be his baby instead?

"Connor was the only man I didn't use protection with, and a few weeks after we broke up, I found out I was pregnant," Cam explained, almost as if she'd read Julia's mind.

Great! And now I've been gifted with an image of Connor and Cam having unprotected sex.

Clearing his throat noisily, Connor said, "That was a mistake."

Julia gaped at him. She understood what he meant, but how could he say that about the beautiful child he'd created?

"I meant…"

"She knows what you meant, Connor," Cam said with a frown.

"So, why come forward now?" Julia blurted out. Ava had to have been at least three months old, or maybe even older. Why had Cam waited so long to tell him?

Inhaling deeply, Cam resumed her explanation. "I didn't want to believe it at first, but after the doctor confirmed it, I realized I had some decisions to make."

Julia's eyes widened, thinking the worst.

"Not that," Cam said. "I knew I was going to keep the baby, but I wasn't sure what to do about telling Connor. I don't know what he's told you, but we had an ugly breakup. I wasn't sure he'd even want to be part of this baby's life."

On cue, Ava cooed and flapped her arms as if to say, "Look at me. Aren't I cute?"

Julia had an overwhelming urge to hold her, but she didn't dare suggest it. There were still too many unanswered questions.

"Anyway, I made the decision to raise the baby myself, thinking that I would be up to the challenge. Turns out, I wasn't. Shortly after Ava was born, I went out to Denver to stay with my sister for a while. She's a stay-at-home mom with two kids of her own, and she offered to help until I decided what to do next. While I was there, my sister convinced me to tell Connor. She made me realize that it was selfish to keep Ava away from her father, and honestly, I could use his help."

That, Julia could understand. Her friends who had children often complained about how much work was involved, especially when they were working parents. So far, it was the one sentence Cam had said that made sense, but Julia still questioned her motives. Was Cam trying to win Connor back? Did she want them to be a family?

Connor shifted uncomfortably as he joined in the conversation. "Cam called me a few weeks ago and told me the news. At first, I wasn't sure what to do, but then I decided to fly out to Denver to…"

"Make sure Ava was really his," Cam finished.

"The minute I saw her, I knew. And then I convinced Cam to come back to Michigan so we can work something out. I'll have to juggle my work schedule, but I'll help whenever I can."

"Juggling is what I've been doing for the past five months," Cam said pointedly.

"If I'd known about Ava from the beginning, I would have been there," Connor argued.

For some strange reason, Julia found herself playing referee. "Okay, you two. The past is the past. The question is, what happens now?"

"I'm not sure," Cam said. "I gave up my apartment when I went to Denver. I can stay with my parents for a while, but I need a more permanent solution. Otherwise, I'll go back to Denver, where I know I'll have help."

"We've already discussed this. You're not going back to Denver," Connor said adamantly.

Julia looked between them and wondered how this could have happened. Well, she knew how, but why? Why hadn't they used protection like responsible adults? Connor had always insisted on using protection with her.

"Isn't there anyone else who can help you?" Julia asked.

"My parents have health issues, so I don't want to burden them, and I don't have any other close family nearby. That's why I went to Denver in the first place," Cam said.

"What about daycare?" Connor interjected.

"I hate the thought of leaving Ava with a stranger all day. Besides, I have friends who use daycare, and their kids are always sick. I don't want to subject our baby to that."

It was the same refrain Julia had heard from other parents, and she'd empathized with them.

Looking at the precious bundle in Cam's arms, she could understand why it would be difficult to leave her. But the phrase "our baby" had taken her aback, and she wondered how long it would take for the reality to sink in.

In the meantime, Cam was still talking. "My boss said I could work from home a couple days a week, but I still have to figure out what to do with Ava on the other three days."

"Big of him," Connor said sarcastically.

"None of this is his fault, Connor. This was all you and me," Cam snapped.

Julia cringed, realizing that Cam was still working for the man she'd had an affair with. She was teetering between feeling sorry for their predicament and feeling like she wanted to bolt out the door, shocked that she'd become caught up in this crazy situation. Yet something inside her kept her rooted to the spot, and she was even considering ways that she could help. *Now who's the crazy one?*

Connor scratched the back of his neck, his nervous tell, and said, "I told you I'd think of something. Just give me some time. But I know one thing for sure. You're not taking Ava back to Colorado. She's my responsibility too, and I'll do my part."

At that moment, Julia was proud of him. Even though she could see how uncomfortable he was, he wasn't about to cut and run. Reliability was a trait that all three O'Brien brothers possessed, and she admired them for it. The only ingredient that was missing here, and perhaps the most important, was love. But Connor had just discovered that he was a father. How could he love someone that he didn't even know yet?

"I might be able to help too," Julia blurted out—again. *When will I ever learn to keep my mouth shut?*

Connor and Cam turned and stared at her.

"What I mean is, maybe I could babysit sometime."

Softening, Connor said, "Julia. You don't have to do this."

"I know that. I'm offering."

Placing his hand on her arm, he said, "Thank you," while Cam looked on with a disgruntled expression.

Julia saw relief and tenderness in his eyes, but sadly, she didn't share the same feelings. It still stung that he hadn't told her about Ava sooner. She imagined he'd been shocked by the news, but still. Relationships were built on mutual respect and trust, and if he hadn't trusted her enough to tell her—well, what did that mean for them? And if she hadn't shown up today, when would he have told her? Was he considering getting back together with Cam? Is that why he'd kept Julia out of the loop? The issues they'd dealt with up until now seemed minuscule compared to this, and she wondered how or *if* they'd get past it.

"Connor? I think Ava's wet. Would you mind taking her into the spare room and changing her?" Cam asked.

Connor stood and said, "Sure. I could use the practice."

"Thanks," Cam said, handing Ava to him. "The diaper bag is by the door."

Julia watched him walk away with Ava cradled in one muscular arm, and she couldn't help but smile. *Connor will make a good father. He just doesn't know it yet.*

"You're smiling," Cam stated after he'd disappeared from view.

"Yes. I guess I am."

"I wouldn't have expected that."

"I love babies."

"Do you love him too?"

Julia stiffened, one, because she couldn't believe Cam's boldness, and two, because it was too soon to be talking about love and Connor in the same sentence, especially after what had just transpired. "I…uh. You know what? That's really none of your business."

"Fair enough. It's just that I noticed the way you two look at each other, and I wondered if it was serious. Well, serious for Connor, anyway."

Julia darted a glance down the hall, and when she was sure that it was empty, she said, "What is that supposed to mean?"

Flipping her long blonde hair off her shoulder, Cam replied, "It's just that I can't imagine Connor settling down with anyone. That's why I didn't come running to him when I found out I was pregnant. I didn't think he'd want to be saddled down with a wife and baby."

"Wife? After what you did, who could blame him?"

"You don't know the whole story."

"I know enough, and I know that Connor might have stayed loyal to you if you'd have done the same."

Cam winced, but then they heard footsteps, and they stopped talking.

"Good as new," Connor said, holding Ava up in the air. He must have been proud of the job he'd done as he hadn't bothered to put Ava's pants back on.

Julia took one look at Ava's diapered bottom and started laughing. Cam tried to remain stoic, but soon she was laughing too.

"What?" Connor asked, looking dumbfounded.

"You put it on backwards!" Julia exclaimed, and she immediately jumped up to assist; however, Cam beat her to it. It was like Cam was trying to stake her claim on her daughter, and maybe on Connor too.

Rubbing her hand along Connor's bare forearm, Cam said, "That's okay. You'll learn." And then she took Ava out of his arms, along with the diaper bag and her pants, and left to fix the mistake.

It was the first moment they'd gotten alone, and Connor looked more nervous than he had before.

Shoving his hands in his pockets, he said, "I'm sorry about all this. I don't know what else to say except that I'm really sorry."

"I don't understand why you didn't tell me sooner. Maybe I would have gone to Denver with you."

"Why would you have done that?"

"Because that's what couples do, Connor. They work together. They help each other. They share things with each other, especially huge, important things like this."

Connor cast his eyes downward for a moment, but he didn't have time to respond because Cam and Ava came back into the room.

"I guess you two have a lot to talk about. We should probably go," Cam said.

And then it happened again. Julia's mouth opened, and the words just tumbled out. "Or you could leave Ava here for a little while. I'm sure you have some errands to do or something."

Cam eyed her disbelievingly, and Connor's expression morphed from shock to gratitude.

"You know what? I wouldn't mind a little more time with Ava so we can get to know each other," he said.

Cam looked like she was about to protest, but then she decided not to. "Okay, I guess. Since we just changed her, she should be good for a while."

"What about food?" Julia asked.

"There's a bottle in the fridge. If she seems hungry, you can just warm it up."

"Great. Is there anything else we should know?" Julia said.

"I don't think so. She's pretty easy. As long as she's fed and dry, she should be fine."

"Must take after me," Connor joked, but neither of the women laughed. Cam was attempting to juggle the baby while putting on her jacket at the same time, and Julia stepped forward to help.

"Here. I'll take Ava," Julia offered, holding out her arms.

Cam hesitated for a moment before reluctantly transferring the baby to Julia. Connor held the front door open for Cam, who said a quick goodbye and promised to be back within an hour or two. After Cam left, Julia felt some of the tension drain out of her. And with Ava's sweet little face staring up at her and her pliant, warm body nestled against her, how could she be uptight?

A baby. Something she'd always wanted. Soft, cuddly, and adorable and—*not hers*. She would do well to remember that.

Chapter 2

Shortly after Cam left, an uncomfortable silence settled over them. Well, except for Ava, who seemed content in Julia's arms, babbling and cooing at nothing. They sat back down on the couch, but Connor didn't make a move to take the baby, so Julia continued to hold her and waited for him to speak.

"God, this is overwhelming," he said, shoving his hands through his hair.

Julia felt the same way, and there were still nagging questions that she wanted answered.

"Do you think you'll be able to prevent Cam from taking Ava back to Colorado?"

"I don't know. I'm not sure what my rights are in this situation."

"Me either since the two of you aren't married." Imagining him and Cam having sex was bad enough, but thinking about them getting married...

"That'll never happen," Connor said adamantly.

"I wonder if that's what Cam's hoping for."

"Doesn't matter. It's not going to happen."

Julia nodded, but she still felt uncertain. If he and Cam were married, there wouldn't be a custody issue. The way things stood, what was to prevent Cam from taking off with the baby if she really wanted to?

"Ahbahbah," Ava cooed, disrupting Julia's train of thought.

Turning her around, Julia held Ava up and took a long look at her. How was it possible that she could already see so much of Connor in her? His steely blue eyes, his perfectly oval face, and his straight nose were all evident. Ava didn't have much hair yet, but what she did have was light brown, the combination of her parents' hair colors. Regardless of what her final hair color turned out to be, she was sure to be a stunner. Even though Julia hated to admit it, Cam was a strikingly beautiful woman, and Connor, well...

"What are you thinking?" he asked, breaking into her thoughts.

"Oh, just how pretty she is."

"Yeah," he said, "she is, isn't she?"

"Do you want to hold her now?"

"Sure."

Once Ava was settled between his large hands, she gazed at him almost as if she recognized their connection. Was that even possible? Could Ava sense that this man was her daddy? She reached out her chubby little fist and batted his face, and Connor laughed.

"You're not the only woman who wants to hit me," he teased, glancing over at Julia.

For a few minutes, she'd been able to forget about her anger, but now that he'd brought it up...

"You're right about that," she confirmed.

"How can I make it up to you?"

"You can start by explaining why you didn't tell me about Ava when you first found out."

Ava started fussing then, and Connor looked panicky. "What should I do? Do you think she's hungry?"

"Hold on," Julia said. "Let me see if Cam packed any toys in the diaper bag." Rummaging through the bag, she came up with a rattle, a stuffed bear, and a teething ring. "Here, let's try these first."

Connor took the rattle from her and shook it in front of Ava's little face. Her frown turned upside down, and she seemed pleased again.

"See. It's not so hard," Julia said.

"Maybe not for you, but this stuff isn't instinctual for a man."

"You'll learn," she said, realizing that Cam had said the same thing while caressing Connor's arm.

"To answer your question, I freaked. When Cam called and told me, I didn't believe her at first. But then she sent me some pictures, and it was obvious that Ava was mine."

"And you have no doubts? What about Cam's boss?"

"That's impossible."

"Why?"

"Because he's black."

"Oh." Now she understood why Cam and Connor had been so adamant about Ava's parentage. Ava's skin was milky white.

"And the timing makes sense. Cam said she hadn't slept with anyone other than me and Tyler, her boss, and I believe her."

"Is she still seeing him? Personally, I mean."

"I'm not sure."

"Hmm." There went any hope that this had all been a mistake. As cute as Ava was, Julia didn't enjoy the thought of her being the catalyst that brought Connor and Cam back together.

"Hey," he said as if he could read her troubled mind. "There's no reason for you to be worried about this. I have zero interest in getting back with Cam."

"Yes, you've said that. However, she is the mother of your child, and that means she's back in your life to stay."

Connor scowled. "Well, when you say it like that…"

"You still haven't completely answered my question. After you saw the pictures of Ava, why didn't you come and tell me instead of acting all secretive and running off to Colorado?"

"I guess I felt like it was something I had to do alone. When I went there, I didn't even have a plan. I just wanted to talk to Cam and see Ava. But after I spent some time with her, Ava that is, I couldn't imagine coming home without her."

"And Cam too."

"Like you said, she's Ava's mom. I couldn't just take off with Ava and leave her there."

"Why not? That's what she did to you." Julia hated how petty she sounded, but she couldn't help it. Her emotions were all over the place.

"I didn't ask for any of this to happen, Jules."

"Yet you didn't use birth control."

"I already said that was a mistake."

"Funny, you never made that mistake with me." *And now I sound like a bitch!*

Shaking his head, he traded the rattle for the teething ring, which Ava immediately stuffed into her mouth. "I don't know what I was thinking back then."

"Or maybe you were so caught up in the heat of passion that you forgot. Is that it?" Now that she'd gone down this path, she'd gotten even more fired up.

"Julia."

"Don't Julia me. I have every right to be upset. First, I find out my boyfriend has been keeping a huge secret from me, and then I have to accept that he has a baby with his ex-girlfriend who he once *loved*. So, what? Am I just supposed to sit back and go along for the ride? Is that it?"

Just then, Ava started fussing again, and deciding she needed a break, Julia stood up. "Stay here," she demanded when Connor started to get up. "I'll warm the bottle and be right back."

Once she was out of sight and had put the formula in the microwave to warm, she leaned against the kitchen counter and breathed deeply. She still couldn't believe this was happening. Why was it that just when they'd overcome one obstacle, they encountered another one? And in this case, the obstacle was in the form of a baby who was crying in the next room. Poor child. She had no idea what kind of havoc she'd created, and yet, none of it was her fault. She was innocent in all this, and that's what made the situation even more difficult. If Ava had been Connor's niece, cousin, or a friend's baby, Julia would have been thrilled to help him babysit. But this wasn't babysitting. This was a commitment. Ava would always be part of Connor's life, and now Julia's too as long as they were together.

"Jules? Is the bottle ready yet?" Connor called.

She'd been so lost in thought she hadn't realized that the microwave had pinged. "Let me check," she replied. Testing the formula on the inside of her wrist, she determined that it was the right temperature and hurriedly returned to the living room. It was hard to ruminate over her own problems when there was a hungry mouth to feed.

Connor was pacing the room and patting Ava on the back as he tried to soothe her. For a second, it stopped Julia in her tracks—the vision of this big, muscular man cradling a tiny baby. Even though he looked like an inexperienced new dad, she still found the scene breathtakingly beautiful.

"Jules? You gonna give me that?" he said, holding his hand out for the bottle.

"Yeah. Sorry," she said and handed it to him.

The instant Ava's mouth closed around the nipple, she quieted. And then the vision of daddy and daughter became even more tender.

Connor continued to stand, but he rocked Ava gently in his arms as he fed her, staring down at her with a look of wonder on his chiseled face.

Suddenly, Julia felt like an intruder. Like she shouldn't be the one witnessing such a tender moment. Cam should.

Connor hadn't even looked in Julia's direction since she'd given him the bottle, so he hadn't seen her eyes tear up. Turning away, she started stuffing Ava's toys back in the diaper bag. Once she'd finished, she said, "You know what? I'm going to leave and let you two have some quiet time."

His head jerked up, and he looked panicky again. "What? No. Don't leave. We're not done talking yet."

Giving him a half-smile, she said, "We can talk more later. Cam will probably be back soon, and you need some bonding time with your baby." She sounded more confident than she felt and hoped Connor was buying it.

He peered at her for a few seconds and then sighed. "You're probably right, but what if she gets fussy again?"

Julia raised her brows. "She looks pretty content to me."

Ava was peacefully sucking on the bottle, and her little eyes had started to close. But sensing that Connor needed her, Julia was hesitant to leave.

"When she's done eating, you need to burp her."

"Terrific. How do I do that?"

"Have you had *any* experience with babies?"

"Little to none."

"Okay. Well, just hold her up on your shoulder and pat her back gently yet firmly until she burps. It's pretty simple."

"Got it. Hold, pat, burp," he chanted.

Julia couldn't help but laugh even though her stomach was still tangled up in knots. If nothing else, it might be fun to watch Connor navigate parenthood.

"What if she doesn't burp?" he asked.

"That's okay. Just keep her upright for a while after she's done eating."

"How do you know so much about babies?" he asked.

"My dad's a pediatrician, remember? I've been around babies my whole life."

"It shows."

"If you think flattery will get me to stay longer, you're wrong."

"Can't blame a guy for trying."

But she could blame a guy for knocking up his ex-girlfriend and turning their lives upside down. *Get a grip, Julia.*

"If Cam doesn't come back soon, you might want to check Ava's diaper again. Don't be surprised if it's messy, since she just ate."

Connor wrinkled his nose. "Are you sure I can't convince you to stay?"

And there was the million-dollar question. Part of her really wanted to, but part of her felt like leaving was the right thing to do. As much as she felt upended by this, Connor must have been feeling it tenfold. She didn't plan to abandon him permanently, but she needed some space too. He wasn't the only one who needed to process this.

As if he realized it too, he said, "Never mind. I'll be fine. But let's talk soon, okay?"

"Okay," she said. Connor started to follow her toward the front door, but she put up a palm to stop him. "You should keep her away from the door. It's chilly out today."

"Oh. Right," he whispered.

She shot him a brief smile and then walked outside into the crisp, fresh air. The wind hit her like a slap in the face, but she welcomed it. She'd felt warm and clammy inside Connor's house, and now she released the tension in her neck and shoulders. *Yes. Leaving was the right decision*, she thought as she drove away. But why did she feel so empty?

The empty feeling presided over the next few days, when neither she nor Connor bothered to contact each other. Since he'd missed a few days of work when he'd gone to Colorado, she assumed he'd be working a lot to make up for it. But that didn't answer what he was doing with the other hours of his days. *Probably spending them with his daughter and ex-girlfriend,* she'd reminded herself countless times.

She'd been going over the entire scenario in her head when Harper interrupted. "Jules? You okay? You've been staring at the same screen for ten minutes straight."

"Oh. Sorry. I don't know where my head's at today." *Or the last three days for that matter.*

"Everything okay with Connor?"

His name was bound to come up some time, but Julia didn't have a good answer.

"Eh," she said.

"Well, that doesn't sound very promising."

"Tell me about it."

"Why don't you tell me?"

Since Harper hadn't mentioned anything about Connor's daughter, Julia assumed he hadn't told his brothers yet. *Typical Connor, still keeping secrets.*

"We're having some…issues right now, but I'm sure we'll work it out." *Will we? Do I even want to?*

"Have you talked to him about it?"

"Some, but we haven't resolved anything yet."

"Stubborn O'Briens. Finn's the same way," Harper said with a gleam in her eye. For a moment, Harper's happiness took Julia's mind off her own problems. Harper practically floated around the photo studio these days, and she was always in a hurry to leave so she could see Finn.

Julia had experienced the same feeling with Connor, as fleeting as it had been. Now she wondered if she would ever feel that way again.

"Don't give up on him," Harper said. "I almost did with Finn, but I'm so glad I didn't."

"Yes, but Finn's different."

"They're not that different."

"But your relationship started off differently. You two were friends for a long time before anything happened. I can't say the same for me and Connor. I didn't even like him at first, and the next thing I knew, we were lovers."

"Every relationship follows its own path. There is no right or wrong. It can still work, Jules."

"Have you been reading self-help books again?" Julia teased. But before Harper could answer, her cell phone rang, and when she glanced down at the screen, her entire face lit up.

"Don't worry about me," Julia said. "Go. Take your call."

Harper blew her a kiss and walked out the door of the studio, saying, "Hey, Finn."

After work, Julia dreaded the thought of driving home to an empty house. Funny how, before she'd started dating Connor, the silence hadn't bothered her. But without him, she felt more alone in her house than ever. She was contemplating how to spend the rest of her evening when she turned the corner onto her street and saw a familiar sight— Connor's Jeep parked in her driveway. And when she looked up toward her house, there he was, sitting on her front porch with his head bowed and his hands clasped, almost like in prayer.

When she clicked the garage door opener, his head popped up, and he broke into a wide smile. If she'd been tangled up in knots before, the feeling was magnified now. His smile wormed its way into her heart and made her realize that she wasn't done with Connor O'Brien yet. Not by a long shot.

Chapter 3

He couldn't help it. The minute he saw Julia whip around the corner in her bright-red Mini Cooper, he broke out with a huge grin. The car was small, sporty, and fun, just like her. Once he'd gotten to know her, he'd discovered it suited her to a tee. Practical yet sassy, and never to be underestimated, which reminded him of their first date…

"What are you doing here?" Julia asked when he showed up at the photo studio one evening.

"I hope someday I'll get a better greeting than that," Connor said, his eyes twinkling with humor.

"That's something you'll have to earn," she said and started to walk away from him.

"Hey. Where are you going?" he asked, placing his hand on her arm to stop her.

"Home. Why?"

"What about that drink?"

Julia gaped at him like he had two heads. "Tonight?"

"Yeah. That's what we said."

"As I recall, we never agreed on a day or time."

"That's not how I see it. You asked me if I wanted to go out for a drink, and I said…"

"Hell yes," she finished. "I fail to see where that sentence contains a date or time."

Connor tipped his head back and laughed. "Oh, so you're one of those women, huh?"

"One of what women?"

"The kind who have to have everything spelled out. What was I supposed to do, send you a written invitation?"

Draping her purse over her shoulder, she punched her hands on her hips and said, "A simple phone call would have sufficed."

Studying her for a few seconds, he changed tack. "Okay. Look. I made a mistake. How about if we start over?" And then, without waiting for a response, he said, "Hey, Julia. Would you like to go out and have a drink with me tonight?"

She debated it for what felt like a long time before answering, "Okay."

"Cool," he said, and they both started walking toward the driveway. Connor had purposely blocked in her Mini Cooper with his Jeep, but she took out her keys anyway. Confused, he said, "That's okay. I'll drive."

Tossing her purse into the passenger seat, she leaned against the door frame and scowled at him. "You're right. You'll drive *your* Jeep, and I'll follow you in *my* car."

He was about to protest, but then he just flung out his arms and said, "Okay. Fine. I'll meet you there." And then he turned and started to walk away.

Julia cleared her throat loudly until he turned back around.

"Now what?" he asked, exasperated.

"Where is there?"

"If you're following me, then you'll find out when we get *there*."

Eyes locked, they held a silent standoff until Julia finally gave in. "Fine, but it better not be your place, because we never agreed to that!"

"You wish," he said and then hopped into the Jeep before she could say another word.

He drove to O'Malley's Bar and Grill, a small mom-and-pop establishment that everyone who lived in the area was familiar with. Having grown up in Brandon, Connor embraced the small-town vibe. And when he got restless, it was a relatively short drive to get to the busier communities of metro Detroit.

When they arrived at the restaurant, he noticed she parked a few spaces away from him, probably thinking it would give her a buffer zone when they left later. *Silly woman.* By the time she'd retrieved her purse from the passenger seat and was about to exit the car, he was already opening her door. See that? He could be a gentleman when he wanted to be.

Looking surprised, she said, "Thank you."

"Welcome. See how easy it is to be nice to each other?"

"The night is young," she said with an eye roll.

Instead of retorting, he placed his hand on the small of her back and led her inside the restaurant. Somewhat surprised she hadn't swatted his hand away, he soaked up the feeling of her warm skin through her top, wondering what it would feel like underneath. Inwardly cursing, he reminded himself to be good. Julia was obviously still wary of him, and he didn't want to scare her away, especially on their first date.

His friend Matt was standing behind the check-in desk when they walked in. "Hey, Connor. Good to see you, buddy."

"You too," Connor replied, reaching around Julia to shake Matt's hand.

"Would you like a table for you and your lovely date?"

Connor had just opened his mouth when Julia butted in. "We're not dating. And we'll just sit at the bar. Thanks."

Wide-eyed, Matt said, "Whatever the lady wants." And then he led them to the bar, where he set down two menus.

After he'd walked away, Connor turned toward her and said, "Are you going to loosen up or what?"

"Huh?"

"You practically bit the owner's head off."

Eyebrows raised, she stammered, "The…the…owner?"

"Yeah, and he was just trying to be friendly."

Julia sighed. "Oh God. I sounded like a bitch, didn't I?"

"Your words, not mine."

Sighing, she said, "I'm sorry. I didn't mean to embarrass you."

And then the bartender came over. "Hey, Connor. What can I get you?"

Connor knew everyone who worked there, and Julia visibly shrank down in her seat.

"I'll take a Guinness and a shot of whiskey."

"And for the lady?"

"I'll just have water."

Connor stared at her, as did the bartender. When they'd agreed to go out for a drink, he hadn't expected her to order water. That didn't even count as a drink in his book, especially not at O'Malley's, where they had an extensive menu of *real* drinks to choose from.

As if she realized her mistake, she said, "Okay, fine. I'll have a shot of whiskey too."

She looked pleased with herself, and Connor chuckled.

"What?" she said.

"Just curious. Have you ever had a shot of whiskey before?"

Julia thought about it for a few seconds and replied, "I'm not sure. Maybe once, in college."

"Hmm."

"Hmm, what? You don't think I can hold my liquor?"

"I guess we'll see. Maybe we should order dinner too."

"I agreed to a drink, not dinner," she huffed.

"Fine. How about an appetizer?"

Finally, she agreed. When the bartender returned with their drinks, Connor put in an order for not one, but three different appetizers.

"We might as well have ordered dinner," she scoffed.

Ignoring her, he held up his shot glass and said, "You ready?"

She looked nervous for a moment but then said, "I guess so."

"On the count of three. One…two…three."

Julia's reaction was comical. She sputtered, her face wrinkling up like a rotten banana and her hands clutching the edge of the bar in a death grip.

"Good, huh?" he said, taking great pleasure in her reaction.

It took a minute for Julia to be able to speak, and then she said, "Yeah. Really good." When she licked her lips as if to confirm it, Connor felt a twitch down below. *Down, boy.*

"One more before the food comes?" he asked.

Eyeing him skeptically, she said, "Are you trying to get me drunk?"

He laughed. "If I was, I wouldn't have ordered any food. It's up to you. No pressure."

He watched as she contemplated the offer, wondering what she was thinking. He didn't know that much about her yet, but he suspected that she was a rule follower. He might even have called her uptight until now, when she'd finally started to loosen up. Surely, the liquor helped, but he hoped that some of it was due to him. He didn't want her to feel nervous with him. He'd much rather she be relaxed and have fun. Surely, there'd be no harm in that.

"Okay. Just one more," she said.

Trying not to act surprised, Connor ordered the second round, which they downed right before the appetizers came. She seemed to handle the liquor a lot better the second time, and when she looked at him afterward, her eyes were sparkling.

"So, tell me a few things I don't know about Julia Lee," he said in between bites of the oversized Bavarian pretzel they were sharing.

"I'm an only child," she blurted out as she dunked a hunk of pretzel in the gooey cheese sauce. "And I really want kids someday—like three or four. Oh, and a dog, because I don't like cats."

34

His hand froze over the cheese sauce. "Okay, then. That's…"

"Crazy? At least that's what Alec said."

"Who's Alec?"

"My ex. We talked about getting married, but then he casually mentioned that he didn't want kids—ever."

"Ouch."

"Yeah. So, that was a deal-breaker for me. What about you?"

He was cutting into a loaded potato skin and didn't look up. "Three or four kids sounds like a lot, but I suppose it's doable."

Julia stared at him, her mouth agape. "That's not what I was asking!"

"Oh. Sorry. I must have lost the thread of the conversation," he teased.

"I was turning the question around on you. What can you tell me about Connor O'Brien that I don't already know?"

"That depends. What do you think you know about me?"

"I know that you're the middle of three brothers and that you're the bad boy of the bunch."

He set down his fork and looked directly at her. "Did somebody tell you that, or is that your opinion?"

Julia shrugged. "A little bit of both, I guess. I've overheard a few comments from Finn, and I've also seen you in action."

Leaning closer, he whispered, "You haven't seen anything—yet."

His thigh brushed against hers underneath the bar, but he didn't move away, and neither did she. The thought of that pleased him to no end. Maybe he was finally getting to this girl. This girl who drove him crazy with desire and something else too. She might act all tough, but he saw glimpses of her vulnerability too, and it made him want to protect her. To hold her, kiss her, possess her, and take care of her all at the same time.

"Hmmm," she said while spearing a mozzarella stick.

"Hmmm, what?"

"Just wondering if you're all talk and no action."

And now it sounded like she was goading him! "When you're ready to find out, you just let me know."

"Can I get you two anything else?" the bartender asked, startling them. They'd been gazing into each other's eyes and hadn't heard him approach.

"Julia? Another drink?" Connor asked.

"No!" she practically shouted. And then, lowering her voice, she said, "No thank you."

They reached for the bill at the same time, their hands touching briefly as he swooped it out from under her.

"I got it," he said, pulling his wallet out of his back pocket.

"Oh, no you don't," she said, reaching into her purse. "This wasn't a date, and in modern times, women split the bill."

"There's something to be said about the old days," he muttered. Slapping down some money on the bar, he grabbed her arm and practically pulled her off the stool. "Thanks, Ed," he called over his shoulder to the bartender, and then keeping his hand clamped around her arm, he led her out of the restaurant.

He hadn't meant to manhandle her that way, but she didn't pull out of his grip, so maybe she hadn't minded. God, this woman was confusing, shooting him down one minute and then heating under his gaze the next. She was a puzzle he definitely wanted to solve.

It was dark out, and the temperature had cooled off significantly compared to when they'd arrived. He walked her to her car, and as she dug through her purse for the keys, she shivered.

"Where's your coat?" he asked, sliding his hands up and down her arms to warm her.

"I left it at the studio. It was warmer earlier," she said, averting her eyes.

Deciding he'd touched her enough for tonight, he dropped his hands and took a step back. "You okay to drive home?"

Raising her brows, she said, "I didn't drink *that* much. Besides, you filled me up with enough appetizers to absorb all the alcohol."

He chuckled, and then they just stood there and stared at each other for a moment.

"Thank you for paying," she said.

"I'd do it again."

"What, pay?"

"Well, you'd have to go out with me again, but yeah, that too."

"Are you asking me out again?"

"Sounds like it."

Julia giggled and shook her head. "You're a hard man to read, Connor O'Brien."

"Not really. Not with a little practice."

And then he stepped forward, reached out, and fingered a lock of silky black hair that was curling softly over her shoulder. "What do you say?"

As he twirled her hair around his fingers, he wondered what it would look like splayed on his pillow with her naked and writhing beneath him. Once again, he wondered what she was thinking and why she hadn't stopped him. He'd taken a few liberties tonight, and he'd kept waiting for her to throw the hammer at him, yet she hadn't. Maybe she was warming up to him after all.

Looking up at him in the darkness, she said, "Yes," but added, "I guess so," as though she wanted him to know that she wasn't one hundred percent sold on the idea.

Her response struck him as funny, and he tipped his head back and laughed, the sound echoing in the quiet parking lot.

"I'll accept that answer for now," he said, "But someday, you're going to tell me yes without hesitating."

"We'll see," she replied, and then she quickly got in her car and drove away, leaving him standing there staring after her.

As Connor watched her walk toward him now, he longed for her to return his smile, or at least look at him the way she'd looked at him that night. But then, what did he expect? They'd just started getting into a good rhythm with each other when the rug had been ripped out from under them.

A few weeks ago, she would have greeted him with a hug and a kiss (or four), and they would have gone into her house and maybe straight to her bedroom. Or, depending on how hungry she was, they might have eaten first. The woman had a hearty appetite, as he'd quickly discovered. She'd only denied him dinner that first time because she hadn't wanted to admit they were on a date. Since then, she'd never turned him down for dinner again.

He leaned toward her as she came up on the porch, hoping for a kiss, but she turned her head to the side, and he barely grazed her cheek. The move gave him a sense of foreboding, but he plowed ahead.

"Mind if I come in?"

"That depends," she said, her voice cool.

"On what?"

"On what you came over here for."

Sighing, he said, "Maybe I just wanted to see you."

She gazed at him skeptically, but he caught a flicker of hope there too. It was then that he realized he had his work cut out for him. She wasn't about to welcome him into her home, let alone her bed, until he smoothed things over with her. And that's exactly what he'd come there to do.

"Come on, Jules. I think we need to talk, don't you?"

"Isn't it the woman who usually says that?" she asked with a thin smile.

"You could have called me anytime."

"I could say the same to you."

Connor ran a hand through his spiky hair, which was getting a bit longer than he was used to. He'd been so busy since he'd returned from Denver that he hadn't had time to get it trimmed. Denver— the trip that had changed his life forever—some for the good, some for the not so good. Case in point, his relationship with Julia, who stood there staring at him as if she were waiting for something. But what it was, he had no idea.

Finally, as if she'd grown tired of standing on the porch, she said, "You can come in, but we're not having sex."

Biting back a chuckle, he said solemnly, "Understood."

"I mean it, Connor. Don't think you can flash your panty-melting grin at me and expect me to hop into bed with you. I'm still mad at you."

Obviously, he almost said. "Understood," he repeated, but this time, he didn't bother hiding his smile (or his panty-melting grin, as she'd referred to it).

He stood behind her as she inserted her key in the lock, and quietly inhaled her scent—strawberry shampoo and some soft, floral perfume she used. He realized he didn't know the name of it and vowed to find out. He'd been on a mission to find out everything he could about this woman until he'd found out that he was a father. It still astounded him whenever he thought of it, which was constantly these past few days.

"Are you coming in or what?" Julia said as she held the door open for him.

He'd been so lost in thought that he hadn't realized he was still standing on the porch. "Yes," he said, stepping inside. "Thank you."

He wasn't sure what he was thanking her for. Maybe it was for not turning him away, which she very well could have. He hadn't been completely upfront with her, and he regretted that now. Seeing the tight set of her shoulders, and the way she held herself away from him made him angry. Not at her but at himself.

He sucked at relationships. That's all there was to it. He must have done something wrong with Cam to make her turn to another man, and now he'd screwed up with Julia too. But after walking away from Cam, he had no intention of inviting her back into his life. He didn't want to walk away from Julia, and he didn't want her to either.

"Do you want a beer?" she asked as he sat down on the couch. The one they'd made love on more than once.

"Sure, if you do."

Punching her hands on her hips, she cocked her head and said, "And no trying to get me drunk either." This time, she allowed herself to smile fully, and it lit up the room. He watched her walk away, admiring the curve of her backside, thinking about how it felt to cup it in his hands.

Settle down, man. You're lucky she even let you in to talk.

Julia returned with two beers and handed him one before taking a seat on the loveseat opposite him. He was seriously tempted to join her there, but he figured she'd chosen the seat for a reason—to maintain her distance from him. He hated it, but he had to respect her decision, and he promised himself he wouldn't rush things.

Taking a long slug of his beer, he racked his brain for where to begin while she eyed him and waited patiently. The woman was a picture of cool right then, sipping her beer calmly, the other hand resting in her lap, looking like she had all the time in the world.

If he only knew what was really going through her mind...

Chapter 4

God, he looks good. Too good, as usual. His hair was getting longer, and it was standing up in places where he'd run his hands through it. When he'd put the beer bottle to his lips, she'd wished it was a part of her anatomy instead. Any part would do. Damn! She should not be having this kind of reaction to him right now. *You're supposed to be mad at him, remember?*

But she shouldn't have been surprised. She'd always had this kind of response to Connor, even at the beginning, when she was determined not to like him. Looking back, she realized that their relationship had been explosive from the start. Like she'd explained to Harper, they hadn't started out as friends and slowly progressed from there. Rather, she'd avoided him like the plague for weeks until she'd decided she didn't want to anymore. After that, they'd gone from zero to one hundred in no time flat.

The whole thing was mystifying and unlike any relationship she'd had before. Especially with her ex, Alec, where everything had moved along slowly and steadily until it had petered out. She couldn't imagine this thing she had with Connor dying out like that.

Going up in flames, maybe, just like they'd begun. Peering at him over her beer bottle, she remembered what had happened the first time they'd drunk beer together...

The bar/restaurant was already getting crowded, but they managed to find a table that afforded them a view of the stage. While the band members tuned up their instruments, Connor and Julia ordered drinks, but this time, she opted for a beer instead of whiskey, and Connor did the same.

"What do you want to eat?" Connor asked as he perused the menu.

"I'm really not that hungry. I had a late lunch."

He narrowed his eyes at her over the top of the menu. "You got something against dinner?"

Skimming her hands along the sides of her body, she said, "Does it look like I turn down food to you?"

Connor tipped his head back and laughed.

Ignoring him, she said, "I'm not hungry enough for an entire meal, but I'll split something with you."

"Cheeseburger and fries okay?"

"Sure."

After the waitress took their order and left, Julia settled back in her chair and sipped her beer while she watched the band warm up.

"I always thought it'd be cool to play in a band," Connor said.

"Do you have any musical talent?"

"Does singing in the shower count?"

"I think everyone does that."

"Then no. Not one bit!"

She laughed. "I could see you up there with a guitar strapped across your chest, and your tat—" She halted when she saw the way he was looking at her, his eyes lit up with pleasure. Nothing like making it obvious that she'd checked him out.

"You've noticed my tattoo?"

Julia shrugged. "I just happened to notice the edge of it one day when you were working outside at the studio." *Great! Now he's going to think I've been gawking at him out the window.*

"Have you been watching me out your window?"

Julia raised her brows at him. "Don't get cocky. I said I noticed it, that's all."

Thankfully, the lead singer of the band stepped up to the microphone, and they stopped talking as he introduced himself and the other band members before leading into their first song. Shortly after that, the waitress brought over their food, and Julia turned her attention to eating and listening to the music.

The band played several well-known country songs interspersed with some of their own music, and Julia got so into it that she'd started singing a familiar ballad aloud. The song was "Amazed" by Lonestar, and it was one of her personal favorites, so she knew all the words by heart. She hadn't even realized she was singing until she glanced over at Connor and saw him staring. Clamping her mouth shut, she forced herself to stop singing and simply listened to the rest of the song.

When it was over, Connor leaned in and said, "Maybe you're the one who should be in a band. You have a beautiful voice."

Julia shook her head vehemently. "Oh. No. I'm like you. I mostly just sing in the shower."

"Remind me to take a shower with you sometime—just so I can hear your pretty voice again," he said with a wink.

Leave it to him to make it about sex. Although her lady parts didn't seem to think it was such a bad idea. Plus, she'd get to see the rest of his tattoo.

They ordered another beer before the band began playing the second set, and soon a few enthusiastic listeners got up to dance on the small dance floor that faced the stage. Julia admired the dancers, who seemed to lose themselves in the music. Of course, maybe their courage had been alcohol induced. In any case, she was content to sit back, watch, and tap her feet to the rhythm beneath the table.

When the band started playing another ballad, Connor suddenly stood up. Holding his hand out to her across the table, he said, "Dance with me."

He'd formed it as a statement instead of a question, but that didn't change her answer. "No thanks," she said and then took another slug of beer.

Standing firm, arm extended, he said, "Come on, Julia. Take a risk."

She suppressed the urge to shout, "I already am! I'm here with you, aren't I?" Instead, she said, "The dance floor's too crowded."

"We'll find a space. Come on before the song's over."

She'd run out of excuses. Besides, the people on either side of them were watching and waiting to see what she would do. Feeling pressured from all sides, she shoved herself out of the chair and took his hand.

Looking pleased, Connor led her to the edge of the dance floor and settled his hands on her hips. There was an awkward moment where Julia wondered where to put her own hands. Not that she'd never danced with a man before, but this was different. She and Connor weren't a couple, and they weren't in love. They were acquaintances at best.

Seeming to sense her indecision, Connor took her hands and placed them on his chest. And then he pulled her a little closer, to where their hips were almost touching. Still feeling uncomfortable, she ventured a glance at him and saw amusement in his eyes. But this time, instead of feeling irritated with him, she saw the humor in it too. They were both feeling their way with each other. The only difference was that Connor was more of a risk taker than her. In fact, he'd been the brave one all along—asking her out repeatedly even when she'd discouraged him, and now asking her to dance even though he'd probably expected her to turn him down.

The least she could do was enjoy the dance. Moving a step closer, she slid her hands further up his chest until they rested on his shoulders. The man had to be almost six feet tall, so she was grateful for the few extra inches that her cowboy boots afforded her; otherwise, she would have looked ridiculous trying to dance with him.

"That's better," he said, smiling down at her.

While they turned in a slow circle on the crowded dance floor, she became acutely aware of every point where their bodies touched. His arms had encircled her waist, and she felt the hard ridges of his bones beneath the muscle. In the tight space, their chests rubbed against each other, and she felt her nipples harden in response. Good thing the lighting was dim and she was wearing an extra layer.

When someone jostled them from behind, her hips jutted forward and brushed up against the bulge in his jeans. She tried to pretend she didn't notice, but when she glanced up at him, he wore a telltale grin.

"Just ignore him. He's got a mind of his own," Connor teased.

If only it were that easy. There wasn't an ounce of skin, bone, or muscle that she could ignore when they were dancing this close. Luckily, the next song had a fast tempo, so they left the dance floor. They finished their beers quietly after that, but every so often, she'd feel his eyes upon her, and when she locked eyes with him, he didn't bother to look away.

Between the music, the dancing, and the company, all of Julia's senses had come alive, and the air felt charged with possibilities. She hadn't enjoyed herself this much in a long time, and she almost hated for the night to end. It was ten o'clock when they left the restaurant, the music still pumping through her veins along with something else—anticipation, fear, hopefulness? It was likely a combination thereof, and her nerves were thrumming by the time they pulled up in her driveway.

Placing her hand on the car door handle, she hurriedly said, "Well, thanks for tonight. I had a good time." Not waiting for a reply, she started to open the door, but then she realized she'd been talking to an empty space. Connor had already gotten out of the Jeep and come around to her side to open the door and help her out.

"You didn't have to…"

"I wanted to."

They walked up to her door in silence, Connor one step behind her. She didn't look back as she fished her key out of her jacket pocket, inserted it into the lock, and opened it. Once she'd stepped over the threshold, she finally turned around to face him. Bracing his hands on either side of the doorframe, he blocked her view of the outside, but it didn't matter. She knew what was about to happen, but she didn't need the neighbors to see.

Taking a step back, she motioned with her hand and said, "Come on in."

Connor studied her carefully for a few beats before he stepped inside and closed the door firmly behind him.

"Julia? You're staring at me," Connor said, breaking her out of her reverie.

"Just waiting for you to talk," she said.

"Sorry I haven't called for the past few days. I was busy with work, and then I helped Cam get settled into her parents' house."

Julia stiffened. She'd guessed that he'd been spending time with Ava, but she preferred not to think about Cam being there too.

"The thing is, she's not going to want to stay there for long, and I don't blame her. It's not easy moving back in with your parents once you get to be our age."

She wanted to shout, "None of this is easy!" but instead, she just nodded.

"On the plus side, I think Ava's getting used to me being around. She actually smiled at me the other day."

Julia noticed how his face brightened when he said it, and she smiled back. There was no denying that his little girl was adorable.

"Have you told your family about her yet?"

"No, but I plan to this weekend. I've invited them all over on Saturday night, and I'd like you to come too. If you want to," he added.

"Will Cam be there?" She hadn't meant to ask, but as usual, the words slipped out.

Connor shook his head. "I convinced her to let me have Ava for a few hours while she went out with her friends."

Julia tried to hide her relief, but Connor already knew her too well.

"You have nothing to worry about, Jules. It's Ava I'm interested in, not her mother."

"Um-hmm."

Setting his beer bottle on a coaster on the end table (she'd previously trained him on this), he stood up and stalked toward her.

Oh no. It was better when he was across the room from her. She couldn't think straight when he got too close.

Ignoring her distress, or maybe because of it, Connor removed the beer bottle from her clutches and set it down on another coaster. Then, taking both of her hands in his, he pulled her to standing. She didn't bother resisting because she didn't stand a chance against his bulk, but she also didn't immediately melt into his arms.

Holding her hands, he looked down at her and whispered, "I missed you."

Stay strong, Julia. Stay strong.

"I should have told you about the baby before I left for Denver. I regret that now."

She remained silent.

"I've been on my own for so long that I'm not used to sharing things. Hell, I was never that good at it, to be honest. But I'd like to be better—for you."

She'd been staring straight ahead at his chest, and now she glanced up at him to see the sincerity in his expression. But words and actions were two different things, and she questioned his ability to change.

"This whole thing knocked me on my ass, and I didn't want to take you down with me. You shouldn't have to deal with any of this, Julia. You deserve better."

That tripped the switch, and she couldn't stay silent any longer. Jerking her hands out of his grip, she shoved against his chest, but it was like trying to move a mountain. He didn't budge, but he looked at her with surprise.

"You don't get to tell me what I should or shouldn't have to deal with, Connor. That's up to me. I'm not some fragile flower that needs to be handled with care. I'm stronger than that, and if you'd have opened up to me and let me in, you would have realized that."

"You're right."

"And furthermore… Wait…did you just say I'm right?"

Laughing, he said, "You're right, and I was wrong, and I'll keep on saying it until you believe me."

Narrowing her eyes at him, she said, "This doesn't make everything better, you know."

"I know," he said.

"And we still have a lot of talking to do."

"I know that too."

"And you should also know that I'm not happy about Cam being back in your life."

"I'd never expect you to be," he said, reaching out to finger a lock of her hair.

I love it when he does that. "And from here on out, I want to be in the loop."

"Got it," he said, moving his other hand up to cradle her cheek.

Damn. Now I'm doomed. "I don't want you keeping things from me, even things that you think might upset me."

"Noted," he said, rubbing his thumb over her trembling bottom lip.

She shuddered from the touch, her limbs loosening, her brain going numb.

"And?" he said, eyebrows raised.

"And what?"

Eyes sparkling with amusement, he said, "I was just expecting another and."

But she was done ranting. Standing this close, breathing his scent, having his hands on her—he had the same effect he always did.

"And…if we have sex right now, that doesn't mean you're completely forgiven."

He smiled then, slid his arms around her waist, and pulled her close so their hips were touching. "We don't have to do this," he said, giving her the option to change her mind.

Rubbing against his erection, she replied, "You're wrong about that too."

Chapter 5

Connor lifted her up then, and she wrapped her legs around his waist as he carried her down the hall to her bedroom. But unlike the first time they'd had sex, they didn't immediately rip each other's clothes off. This time, his movements were slow, deliberate, and he stripped her defenses with every look, every kiss, every caress.

She needed this, needed him, and she suspected that he needed this too. It was like they were reaffirming the relationship that they'd just started building before it had all come crashing down. When Connor removed his shirt, Julia's hand immediately went to his tattoo, and as she traced the design with her finger, she remembered the first time she'd seen it up close...

Breathing hard, Connor looked down at her and said, "You sure about this?"

"Positive."

Acting like he hadn't heard her, he said, "Because the last thing I want is for you to regret this in the morning."

"No regrets," she said, untucking his shirt from his jeans.

"I mean it, Julia. I'd rather be your friend than have you hate me."

"Who says I'm going to hate you?"

"Just saying."

She'd untucked his gray Henley, and now she slid her hands underneath it, reveling in the feel of his solid, warm chest beneath her fingers. And then she stilled her hands and gazed up at him.

"Regretting it already?" he asked, his voice gruff.

"No. Just wondering if you're going to kiss me or not?"

"That was one of the songs they played tonight," he said as her hands splayed over his chest.

"Just answer the question."

"Hell yeah, I am."

And the next thing she knew, his lips were on hers, capturing her mouth in a searing kiss. She melted into it, letting herself get swept up in the moment. They were slammed up against the front door, her hands roaming under his shirt, when suddenly he cupped her butt cheeks, picked her up, and started walking toward the couch.

"No. Not here," she said, her lust-drunk voice barely recognizable to her own ears. "The bedroom."

Other than the dim light that filtered in through the blinds, it was dark, so she couldn't read his expression, but he halted mid-stride. "I'm gonna ask you one more time…"

"Stop asking. I thought you wanted this."

"I do, but it's you I'm worried about."

"Well, don't be. Last door down the hall on the right."

When they reached her bedroom, Connor let her slide down his body until her feet touched the floor. And it was then that she realized what she was agreeing to. She'd never done this before—invited a man into her bedroom that she wasn't seriously involved with. But something about it felt extremely liberating and right. And it wasn't about Connor and what he wanted. It was about her and what she wanted. Looking at him standing there in the moonlight that was seeping in through the blinds, she was even more sure.

"You gonna stand there and stare, or are we gonna get naked?" he asked, his voice smooth and sexy.

"Oh, we're going to get naked, but you first."

Eyebrows raised, he said, "Whatever the lady wants." And with that, he yanked his shirt over his head and let it fall to the floor.

She saw a glimpse of the black ink on his right bicep as he moved his hands to his belt buckle, and she shivered.

Smiling, Connor continued his striptease, slowly unbuckling his belt and then unfastening his jeans.

Frozen to the spot, Julia waited, and then in a flash, his jeans and boxer briefs hit the floor.

Swallowing hard, she took it all in, letting her eyes leisurely wander over him from head to toe and back again. She'd known he was built from seeing him work outside at the studio. The way his muscles strained and rippled when he'd shoveled mulch or trimmed the trees and bushes. The way his jeans had stretched over his tight butt and rode low on his narrow hips when he'd reached for something. But she'd never seen him like this—erection jutting out proudly, begging for her touch.

He'd let her look, but now he sounded impatient when he said, "Your turn."

Julia wasn't hard-packed like him, but she took care of herself, and she was proud of her curvy figure. She'd expected to feel nervous about getting naked with someone she didn't know that well, but for some reason, she wasn't. The way Connor looked at her when she was fully dressed gave her the confidence she needed to undress before him.

Treating him to the same kind of show he'd given her, she began unbuttoning her shirt and then slipped it off her shoulders. As she was pulling her cami over her head, she heard his sharp intake of breath, and she smiled.

"Damn, woman," he said, zeroing in on her ample cleavage. "Didn't realize you were so…stacked."

Smiling some more, she reached around her back and unclasped her bra, and then she slowly slid down the straps to reveal her full breasts.

Connor took a step forward, looking eager to touch, but she put up a palm and said, "Not yet."

The look he gave her made her feel powerful and in control of the situation instead of the other way around. She wondered for a moment if this was new to him—if he was used to being in charge.

Julia kept her eyes pinned on his as she unfastened her jeans, and hooking her fingers in her panties, she shimmied out of them. It was late fall, and the temperature had gone down considerably, but her body felt like it was burning up under his intense gaze.

And then, two seconds later, they tumbled onto the bed, hands, mouths, and tongues clashing together in a lusty battle where they were both winners.

Julia fully abandoned her cares as he explored her body, palming her breasts in his large, work-toughened hands and then replacing his hands with his mouth, sucking a nipple deep into his mouth and swirling his tongue around it. They were lying on their sides, and she arched her hips forward to rub against his erection as she coiled her arms around his neck and buried her fingers in the soft hair at his nape.

In a quick move, Connor rolled onto his back, taking her with him so she straddled him. Pushing against his chest, she sat up and slid her center back and forth along his hard length while he plucked her taut nipples.

"Not gonna last if you keep doing that," he said gruffly.

"Me neither," she said, her voice fluttery.

Gripping her hips, he lifted her off him and bent over the edge of the bed to retrieve his jeans. While he was rolling on a condom, Julia lay on her back and waited, anxious to have him inside her. But once Connor was sheathed, he leaned over her and ran a fingertip down the center of her body, leaving a trail of goosebumps in its wake.

"So pretty," he said before dipping the same finger into her opening.

"Ahhh," she moaned as he flicked her most sensitive spot.

"Good?"

"Um-hmm."

He kept going, teasing her with one finger and then two, until she squirmed and tightened beneath him.

"Hold that thought," he said, and then nudging her legs wider apart, he entered her, her hips tilting up to receive him.

Once he was fully rooted, there was no stopping either one of them. Holding her head in his hands and locking eyes, he rocked into her with hard, deep thrusts that had the bed groaning under their weight. Soon they came with equal intensity, each of them vocal in their enthusiasm.

Afterward, Connor rolled off her, and she tucked into his side, palm on his chest, as their breathing returned to normal. He played with a lock of her hair, twirling it around his fingers repeatedly, neither of them saying a word.

Finally, after a few more minutes of silence, Connor said, "Be right back."

She watched him pad naked from her bed into the attached bathroom and close the door, and then she pulled a sheet up over her, suddenly cold without his body heat.

Staring up at the ceiling fan, she thought about what they'd done, but amazingly, she didn't have any regrets. She knew what this was about—what he was about—and she was okay with it. True, it wasn't a real relationship, and it might never be, but what was wrong with having a little fun? They were young and single, and nobody was going to get hurt as long as they were open with each other. She could handle this.

And then he padded back in and crawled under the sheet next to her. Propping himself up on an elbow, he peered down at her and said, "Regrets?"

"No."

"Wow. Gotta say I'm a little surprised."

"Why?"

"I didn't expect this to happen tonight."

"But you expected it to happen someday, right?"

Brushing her hair off her shoulder, he said, "I hoped so."

She was surprised too, not just at herself, but at his tenderness. Even though their sex had been—hurried—he'd been thoughtful and considerate, seemingly as interested in giving pleasure as in receiving it.

"I enjoyed it," she said quietly, afraid to give him too many accolades. She was still determined to maintain control of the situation.

He chuckled. "I kind of gathered that."

"What about you?" she asked, turning on her side to face him. She couldn't help but be curious, considering that he'd probably had a lot more sexual experiences than her.

"It was even better than I imagined."

His admission made her heart squeeze along with another part of her, but it was her heart she was worried about. "You probably say that to all the girls."

Shaking his head, he said, "You're wrong."

Since they were venturing into dangerous territory, she decided to change the subject. "Turn your arm this way a little more. I want to see your tattoo."

"It's a compass," he said, twisting his arm so she could see.

Julia ran her fingertips over the ink, tracing the pattern thoughtfully. "What does it mean?"

He laughed. "It doesn't have any deep meaning. I just liked the design."

"When did you get it?"

"A few years ago."

"Hmm. Does it have anything to do with you being adventurous?"

"Maybe. It's kind of like a reminder that there's a great big world out there and you can travel in any direction you want to go."

And now here they were, bringing each other pleasure amidst the uncertainty swirling around them. His body was familiar to her now, but no less exciting. She knew exactly what he liked, and vice versa. And after the slow buildup, when Connor finally slid inside her, she felt her worries disappear.

She let go of the need for control, of her fears about their future, of her worries about his ex-girlfriend reappearing in his life. She simply let herself feel. Running her hands down his broad back, she gripped his buttocks tightly as he thrust into her, and she clenched her sex around him.

Her lips were swollen from when he'd sucked them into his mouth, her skin sensitive where his day-old stubble had rasped against her. His fingers dug into her hips as he picked up the pace, chasing his release as she bucked up beneath him.

And the whole time, he hadn't taken his eyes off her, hadn't allowed his eyes to close. It was like he needed to see her respond to him, needed the affirmation that she still wanted him. And she did. She'd never stopped.

Leaning over her, he paused for a moment and gazed at her, looking like he had something to say. But her body was already too far gone to wait.

"Connor…I need…"

"Tell me."

She wanted to say, "I need you," but instead, she said, "I need to come."

Knowing the best way to get her there, he flipped them over so she was on top. In this position, she controlled the tempo, and it didn't take long before she shattered against him, his climax following right on her heels.

Afterward, she lay tucked into his side, her hand splayed across his chest, his hand stroking her hair. This, she knew. This, she understood. Their physical connection. They'd had it from the beginning, and in that regard, nothing had changed. Although everything had, and she feared their physical connection wasn't going to be enough to propel them forward. But maybe it was a step in the right direction. If nothing else, it had instilled her with a sense of calm that she hadn't felt for the last several days.

"You never answered my question," Connor said, turning onto his side to face her. "Will you come over this weekend when I tell my family?"

"Are you sure you don't want to do it alone?"

"Positive. I'd like you to be there."

"Okay," she said.

Eyes lighting up at her answer, Connor leaned in and softly kissed her. It might have been his form of a simple thank you, but she still felt it all the way down to her toes. Leaning up on her elbow, she looked past him to the clock on her bedside table and was surprised to see how late it was.

"It's getting late," she said.

"Are you kicking me out?" he asked while he traced a circle around one of her exposed nipples.

"No. It's just that we both have to work tomorrow."

Trailing his finger over to the other nipple, he repeated the pattern, seemingly mesmerized by the sight of them hardening in response to his touch.

"I'll leave if you want me to," he said, gliding his hand down the midline of her body and pausing right above her sex.

It probably would have been the wise thing to do, to ask him to leave, but her body disagreed.

"I guess it won't hurt if you stay a little longer," she said breathlessly. *So much for staying strong.*

"I was hoping you'd say that," he said, his hand disappearing between her legs.

And so, they got lost in each other again, using their hands and mouths this time since he'd only brought one condom.

Bodies already primed, they peaked much quicker this time, and after they caught their breath, she said, "Okay. Now you have to leave."

Laughing, he crawled out of bed and started gathering his clothes.

"I'll let you get your beauty rest even though you don't need it. You're already beautiful enough."

She'd been sitting up in bed, sheet tucked around her breasts, watching him dress and already missing him. But for some reason, she kept that little nugget to herself.

"Thank you," she said, beaming at the compliment. He'd told her she was beautiful before, so it was nothing new, but she still liked hearing it.

Funny, Alec had told her the same thing, but his words hadn't had the same effect. Maybe it was because Connor didn't talk as much, so when he gave her a compliment, she knew he really meant it.

"Let me walk you to the door," she said and started to rise.

"No. Stay there. I want to think of you just like that," he said. He'd said the same thing after the first time they'd made love. She wondered if he remembered it too, and based on his grin, she knew he had.

After she heard the front door click shut behind him, she burrowed under the covers and inhaled deeply. She could still smell him and still felt the warmth from where he'd lain. And for the first time since she'd found out about the baby, she fell into a peaceful sleep.

Chapter 6

Connor left Julia's house feeling a helluva lot better than he'd felt for days. And it had nothing to do with getting laid. Of course, that hadn't hurt. He'd gone to her house wondering if she'd even talk to him, with no expectations of having sex. But now his hope was restored that all was not lost.

When she'd agreed to be there when he told his family about the baby, that had been the icing on the cake. He wanted her by his side even though he had no right to expect that of her. When he'd conveyed that to her, she'd gotten mad at him. He smiled remembering how feisty she'd looked with her hands planted on her hips, her deep brown eyes sparking with anger, her full, kissable lips set in a straight line. Even angry, he thought she was the most beautiful woman he'd ever laid eyes on.

And he didn't blame her for being angry—not one bit. This was the second time he'd screwed up in the past few months, and he had a strong premonition that it was three strikes and you're out. He couldn't afford to mess up again. As his Jeep bumped down the dirt road to his house, he recalled their first fight...

"Are you nervous?" Julia asked on the drive over to her parents' house.

"Why do you ask?" he replied without looking at her.

"Because you keep tugging on your collar and there are red splotches all over your neck."

"That's because I'm too damn hot. I never should have worn two shirts."

Since he was meeting her parents for the first time, he'd ditched his faded jeans and long-sleeved t-shirt for a gray crewneck sweater with a collared shirt underneath and black chinos. This was as dressy as he got other than for weddings or funerals.

"Whoa," Connor said when he'd pulled onto the street leading to her parents' house. They lived in an affluent subdivision in nearby Clarkston where the homes looked like manors set back on private heavily wooded lots. This was a neighborhood comprised of doctors, lawyers, and other business professionals who led a privileged life, and this was where Julia had grown up.

"They're just houses," she said.

"Yeah, right."

A few minutes later, Connor followed her up a brick walkway and onto an expansive porch flanked by impressive brick columns. This place was the exact opposite of his childhood home, which was a rambling ranch built in the 1970s and located on a dirt road with farms on either side of it. Glancing at Julia, he realized she was nervous too, which didn't make him feel any better.

"Mom? Dad?" Julia called when they stepped inside.

Seconds later, an attractive middle-aged woman came bustling around the corner, wiping her hands on a black and white checked apron.

"Hi, sweetie. I didn't hear you come in," she said and immediately drew Julia in for a hug. And then Julia turned toward him and said, "Mom, this is Connor."

"Debra Lee. It's very nice to meet you, Connor."

"It's nice to meet you too."

"Come on back to the kitchen. Dinner's almost ready, and Dr. Lee should be here any minute."

He was surprised at Debra's use of her husband's title, but Julia didn't react at all. He got the impression that this dinner was going to be much more formal than his own family gatherings. Growing up in a household with three rowdy boys, there'd been no room for formality. His mom considered dinner a success if he and his brothers kept their hands to themselves and none of them burped at the table.

"Can I get you something to drink, Connor? A glass of wine, perhaps?" Debra said.

Julia must have noticed the slight furrowing of his brows, as she jumped in to say, "Do you have any beer, Mom?"

"Beer? Uh…no. Sorry."

"No problem. I'll just have a glass of water," Connor said.

Looking relieved, Debra turned away to get him a glass of water, and Connor shot Julia a look that said, "See? I don't belong here."

Just as Debra was handing him the glass, the door leading from the garage into the kitchen opened, and in walked Dr. James Lee. His serious expression morphed into a wide smile when he spotted Julia leaning against the kitchen counter, and after giving his wife a quick peck on the cheek, he walked over to greet his daughter.

"Hi, Dad," she said as he embraced her in a tight hug.

At least she didn't call him Dr. Lee, Connor thought.

"How's my baby?" her father asked.

Baby? That cinched it. Everything Connor had perceived about Julia's upbringing was coming true. The fancy house, the successful father, the doting mother. It was all there in black and white. There was no way that her parents would think he was good enough for their only daughter. Her dad still called her "baby," for God's sake!

Instead of responding to her dad's question, Julia said, "Dad, I'd like you to meet Connor."

Dr. Lee had acknowledged Connor with a brief nod when he'd first walked in, but now he let go of Julia and extended his hand.

"Good to meet you, sir...I mean...Dr. Lee," Connor said as they shook hands. He decided to use the title out of respect for Julia, at least until he got to know the man.

Dr. Lee's greeting was friendly enough, but the way he looked Connor over made him uncomfortable. Julia's mom was Caucasian, but her dad was Asian, and he was quite a bit smaller in stature than Connor. Dr. Lee wore a business suit, and Connor was glad that he'd dressed up some, even though he couldn't wait to change back into his jeans and T-shirt. *Does Dr. Lee even own a pair of jeans?* When Connor shook her dad's hand, he couldn't help but notice how smooth and pale it was in comparison to his larger, calloused one. The two men were as different as night and day—there was no way around it.

"If everyone wants to get seated, I'll serve dinner," Debra said, breaking the tension in the room.

"Do you need help, Mom?" Julia asked.

"No, sweetie. You just sit down with your…with Connor."

And there it was—the first hint that Debra was uncomfortable too. Once they were seated, Julia grabbed his hand under the table and gave it a squeeze. He squeezed back, but he kept his eyes focused straight ahead so as not to be accused of making googly eyes at the doctor's daughter.

"So, Connor. What do you do for a living?" Dr. Lee asked while Debra brought plates of food to the table.

"Honey, Julia already told us. He's in landscaping," Debra said.

She might have been trying to save Connor from having to answer, but something about the way she said it didn't sit well with him.

"I'm part *owner* of a landscaping design business," he corrected, "along with my two brothers."

"Ah. I see," Dr. Lee said, helping himself to a scoop of green beans. "Does that keep you busy year-round?"

"Yes, sir. In the winter months, we have contracts for snow-plowing. Living in Michigan, that keeps us pretty busy."

"I'll bet," Debra said as she set a basket of rolls in front of them.

"If you have some business cards, I'll pass them out to some of my friends," Dr. Lee said while cutting into a slab of steak.

Usually, Connor would have welcomed the opportunity to gain more business, but Dr. Lee had sounded patronizing, and Connor didn't want his charity.

"Thanks, but I didn't bring any cards with me," he said and went back to eating.

Sensing the tension in the room, Debra swept in and changed the subject, regaling them with tales from her husband's office, where she worked as his receptionist.

Connor smiled at Debra, thinking how much she reminded him of Julia. They were both petite and curvy, with warm smiles and deep brown eyes, but moreover, it was their personalities that shone. Friendly and open, expressive and engaging, they were quite the opposite of Dr. Lee, whose seriousness made him appear unapproachable and standoffish. Just then, the doorbell rang, startling them all.

Dr. Lee glanced at his watch and then at Debra. "Are you expecting someone?"

"No," she said, "but I'll go see who it is."

After Debra left, Julia stood up and started clearing the dishes, which left Connor at the table with Dr. Lee. Staring at each other across the table, Connor racked his brain for something to say to the man, but thankfully, he was rescued when Debra returned with their visitor. It was a lean young man who looked similar to Julia in that he was a mix of Caucasian and Asian, and Connor wondered if he was a relative. But when he glanced over at Julia, he saw shock and panic on her face and realized that this was nobody she wanted to see.

Honing right in on her, the visitor said, "Hello, Jules."

When Julia didn't reply, the man turned toward the table and said, "Good evening, Dr. Lee."

"Good to see you, Alec. I wasn't expecting you," Dr. Lee said.

Ah-ha. So that's why Julia looks so shaken. She'd told him all about Alec, along with the reason for their breakup. They'd been close to getting engaged when Alec had divulged that he didn't want kids. That had been a deal-breaker for Julia, and as far as Connor knew, she hadn't seen Alec since they'd broken up almost a year ago. Perfect—the evening had just gone from bad to worse.

Debra hurriedly said, "Alec. Meet Julia's friend, Connor."

Roughly pushing back his chair, Connor stood to his full height, and he might have puffed out his chest too.

"Connor O'Brien. Julia's *date*," he said pointedly.

"I see," Alec replied with a forced smile.

Neither of them extended their hands, and Connor sat back down, thinking, *He's the intruder here, not me.*

Clearing his throat, Alec said, "I'm sorry to interrupt. I just stopped by to return the books you loaned me." With that, he handed Dr. Lee the books he'd been carrying.

"Thank you, but you didn't have to make a special trip. We're meeting for coffee next week, right?" Dr. Lee said.

Connor saw Julia stiffen, and it was obvious she'd had no idea that her ex-boyfriend and her father were still seeing each other socially. It took every ounce of willpower he had not to get up, grab her hand, and stalk out of the house. But he waited for Julia to take the lead.

"Yes, sir. But I was in the area, so I'd thought I'd drop by," Alec replied smoothly.

Asshole! Doesn't he realize how awkward this is? Just leave!

"That's okay, Alec. Connor and I were just leaving," Julia said tightly.

"You don't have to leave on my account," Alec said.

"It has nothing to do with you. We have plans this evening," she said and shot him a piercing look.

Connor had left the table to stand beside her, and he slid an arm around her waist for added support. It didn't hurt that Alec noticed the move too.

"Don't you want to stay for dessert?" Debra asked, sounding distressed.

"Yes. And Alec can join us," Dr. Lee added, seemingly oblivious to the tension in the room. Or at least, Connor hoped that was the case. He couldn't accept that her father was doing this on purpose.

"Actually, we have a movie to catch," Connor said. "But thank you very much for dinner."

"Oh. Well, let me walk you out, then," Debra said.

"Have a seat, son," Dr. Lee said to Alec, and the ass, that's exactly what he did.

Dr. Lee stood to say his goodbyes, but Julia motioned for him to sit back down. It was obvious she was just as anxious to leave as Connor was.

Placing his hand gently on the small of her back, Connor guided her out of the kitchen, with Debra following behind them.

Once they were out of earshot and Connor was collecting their coats from the coatrack, Julia turned to her mom and hissed, "Why is he here?"

Sighing, Debra said, "You heard him. He just wanted to return some books to your father. We had no idea he was coming."

"How often does he come over?" Julia asked, her voice shaking with anger.

"Not often," Debra whispered.

In the meantime, Connor was practically shoving Julia's arms into her coat sleeves, and he'd turned her toward him so he could zip up her coat.

Placing a hand on Julia's arm, her mom said, "Your dad is just helping Alec with his studies."

Then she turned to Connor and said, "Thank you so much for coming. I hope we'll see you again sometime."

Nodding, Connor gave her a half-smile and then herded Julia out the door. It wasn't until they were in his Jeep and had pulled out of the neighborhood that she spoke again.

"I am so, so sorry. I had no idea they were still seeing Alec. If I'd have known he'd show up tonight, I never would have brought you there."

Connor gripped the steering wheel tightly, and a vein was pulsing on the side of his neck. Struggling to control his emotions, he said, "It's okay. It wasn't your fault."

When they arrived back at her townhouse, it was still early, and under normal circumstances, he would have wanted to come inside. But he didn't have it in him tonight. Not after all that had transpired at her parents' house.

"Aren't you coming in?" Julia asked.

"Not tonight," he said matter-of-factly.

"Are you upset about Alec showing up?"

"Shit happens."

"That's all you have to say?"

Turning toward her, he growled, "Trust me, you don't really want to hear what I have to say."

"Yes. I really do."

Stubborn woman! Connor sighed and scratched the back of his neck. "Look, Julia. I don't know about this."

"Don't know about what?"

"This. Us."

She gave him a hard stare, but he averted his eyes and continued. "Maybe you were right to stay away from me at the beginning. Maybe this is a mistake."

"You don't mean that. You're just saying that because of what happened tonight. But that doesn't have anything to do with us, Connor."

"You're wrong. It has everything to do with us."

"Why are you doing this? Why are you being such a coward?"

He'd been called worse things, but hearing her accuse him like that flipped a switch inside him. "Go home, Julia."

But she didn't seem fazed by his harsh words, nor the fact that he wouldn't look at her.

"I'm not going anywhere until we finish talking."

"We *are* finished. Go home," he repeated firmly.

"You don't want to talk right now—fine! But we're not done, Connor. You can't get rid of me that easily." And with that, she shoved open the door and stepped out, glaring at him one last time before walking away. He waited for her to go inside and fought the urge to go after her. But once she'd closed the door, he backed out of the driveway and sped off.

It's better this way, he told himself. *She's too good for me. We're too different. It'll never work.*

But here it was a few months later, and they were still together. Julia had forgiven him for driving off in a huff after that night at her parents' house. And he'd forgiven her for calling him a coward, although it still stung whenever he recalled it.

He didn't want her to see him like that. He wanted to be a man she could be proud of even though he'd never be a doctor like her dad or that asshole Alec. No. He'd always choose beer over wine, and a small house in the woods over a mansion in a subdivision. He'd always prefer jeans to dress slacks. But, that didn't make him a lesser man.

He was successful in his own right. He was good at what he did, and not just the physical labor. His favorite part of the job was the design aspect. He found satisfaction in transforming a tangled, weedy, overgrown area into a work of art. He excelled at formulating designs that his customers were happy with. And then, when those plans came to fruition, he felt proud of the hard work he'd done.

Of course, his brothers played a vital role too. Finn was an expert businessman, keeping meticulous records and making sound financial decisions that propelled them forward. Their younger brother, Liam, excelled at building customer relations, marketing, and selling O'Brien Brothers Landscaping to anyone who'd listen. All three of them possessed the brains and the brawn to get the job done.

So, Dr. Lee could look down his nose at him all he wanted. He could have his fancy house, his designer suit, and his professional title. Connor was perfectly content with what he had—a reasonably sized house on ten acres, his Jeep four-by-four, a job that he loved, his family, and a beautiful woman by his side.

Now all he had to do was figure out a way to keep her there.

Chapter 7

Julia showed up early to Connor's house only to find that Cam had beat her there. When Julia peeked in through the screen door, she saw the three of them sitting on the living room floor in a tight circle—Connor, Cam, and Ava. Connor and Cam were laughing as Ava knocked over a stack of blocks, and then Connor built the stack up again.

Since they hadn't noticed her presence, Julia stood there and watched for a moment. If she hadn't known better, she'd have thought she was observing a happy little family. When Ava knocked down the blocks again, Cam placed her manicured hand on Connor's arm and leaned into him.

Okay, that's it! Time to break up this happy little scene.

"Hello. I'm here," Julia announced as she let herself in.

"Julia. Hey," Connor said, rising to greet her.

As he pulled her into a hug, Julia peeked at Cam over his shoulder and saw her glaring at them. But the minute Connor let go, Cam pasted a cheerful smile back on her face.

Ignoring Cam, Julia crouched down, tugged on Ava's foot, and said, "Hello, sweet girl."

Ava smiled and flapped her arms enthusiastically, at which Julia melted and Cam struggled not to frown.

"She likes you," Connor said. "But of course, who doesn't?"

I can think of one person.

"Well, I guess I should go now," Cam said somewhat reluctantly.

"Yeah. I think we can handle it," Connor said, giving Julia a wink.

Cam had been sitting on the floor with her knees tucked underneath her, so Julia hadn't seen what she was wearing until now. When Cam stood, she tugged on her denim miniskirt in a display of modesty. HA! The skirt was so tight Julia couldn't understand how she'd sat down in it. Julia had forgotten how tall Cam was, and she was wearing four-inch wedges that highlighted her long, trim legs. When Cam bent over to say goodbye to Ava, she inadvertently (or maybe not) gave them a full view down her V-neck shirt. Finally, something Julia didn't have to feel jealous about! Cam was taller and leaner than her, but she also had a lot less to show in the breast department. What little she did have was being propped up by a lacy pink push-up bra.

Glancing over at Connor, it was obvious he'd seen down Cam's shirt too. He was busy scratching the back of his neck, his nervous tell.

Cam shot Julia a look of smug satisfaction as she tossed her long blonde hair off her shoulders and then turned her attention to Connor, who was trying to ignore the silent battle that was raging around him.

"I'll be back in a few hours. Call if you need me," Cam said.

As Julia watched her sashay away, she was astonished at how intensely jealous she felt. She never remembered feeling that way with Alec, and he'd been around plenty of other women at med school. But that was different. He hadn't loved any of those women, nor did he have a child with one of them.

"Sorry about that," Connor said after Cam left.

"Sorry about what?" Julia said, sitting down on the floor beside him. It was a warm spring day, but she didn't think it was miniskirt weather. Julia wore cropped jeans and a red crew neck T-shirt, and it struck her that she probably looked more like a mom than Cam did.

"You know," he said as he stacked up the blocks again.

"No, I don't. Tell me."

"Cam. She dresses kind of…"

"Slutty?"

Connor lifted his brows and started laughing. "I was going to say provocatively, but that'll work."

"Has she always dressed like that?" It was hard to believe that Cam was fitting into such skimpy clothes after having given birth five months ago. Julia never expected to be so lucky. Of course, even if she were as slim as Cam, she wouldn't dress like that.

"Yeah," Connor said, refusing to meet her eyes.

"Can I ask you something?"

"Sure," he said warily.

"What did you ever see in her? Besides the obvious, I mean."

Scratching the back of his head, he said, "Honestly? I'm not sure."

"So, it was the obvious, then—the hair, the body, the image." She wasn't sure if that made her feel better or worse, because she was the exact opposite—a blend of her Caucasian and Asian parents. Julia had inherited her dad's silky black hair and her mom's dark-brown eyes and petite, curvy figure. She'd come to accept her curvy body long ago and knew she would never be described as "skinny," but she was okay with that. At least, she was up until now.

"Do you really want to talk about this, Jules? Cam and I were such a long time ago."

"So were me and Alec, but I told you all about him."

Sighing, Connor picked up Ava and held her in his lap, and for a moment, Julia was distracted by what an attractive picture they made. Wait until Harper got a load of this. She'd probably start snapping photos the minute she walked in the door!

"What good does it do to talk about it? It's not like I was excited to hear all about doctor boy."

She laughed. "Doctor boy? Is that the best you could come up with?"

He shrugged. "I can think of a few other choice words…"

"Hmm. So, am I just supposed to ignore the fact that Cam is a beautiful woman who bore your child?"

"Can you?"

"Not a chance."

"Damn it!"

She laughed again but scolded, "Not in front of the baby."

"Uh-oh," Connor said.

"What's wrong?"

"I think she's wet."

"Here. I'll change her this time," Julia said, gently taking Ava out of his arms.

"Thanks. The diaper bag's in the spare room."

Just as they stood up, there came the sound of a car door slamming. *Showtime!*

"It's probably Finn and Harper. He's always early," Connor said.

"I'll hurry," Julia said, responding to the look of panic on his face. "Offer them drinks or something." With that, she rushed down the hall and into the guest bedroom, shutting the door behind her.

The diaper bag was on the bed, and Julia carefully laid Ava down beside it.

"Gagagaga," Ava said as she gazed up at Julia.

"Shhh. Not yet, little one. Save the show for your uncles." *Uncles? Hmm. This ought to be interesting.* Julia and Harper often spoke about the dynamics between the three O'Brien brothers, and Julia wondered how having a new family member would change that. Connor was the prickly one of the bunch, but she'd already begun to notice some changes in him. She'd like to take some of the credit, but she suspected that Ava was the primary reason.

Connor was a father now, and he had more to think about than just himself. He seemed softer, a few of the rough edges having worn off in light of his new role, and maybe that would extend to everyone, even his brothers.

Julia made quick work of changing the diaper and reassembling Ava's clothes. When she picked Ava up, instead of rushing back to the living room, she held her for a moment, enjoying the feel of her in her arms. And then she caught a glimpse of the two of them in the mirror hanging over the dresser and froze. They looked so natural together that she'd almost forgotten that Ava wasn't hers.

"Jules? You can come out now," Connor hollered from the living room.

"Okay, sweetie. Time for your big debut. Knock 'em dead!"

All eyes were upon them as Julia and Ava reentered the living room—Harper's, Finn's, and Liam's, who must have shown up while Julia had been changing Ava. Julia scanned the room for Connor and found him seated in an armchair, hands clasped tightly between his knees and looking nervous. When their eyes met, he smiled and seemed to relax some. Did she really have that kind of effect on him? Maybe he really did need her after all.

Harper was the first to speak, jumping off the couch where she'd been sitting next to Finn and rushing toward Julia and Ava.

"Ohmigod. She's absolutely adorable!" she gushed, reaching out to touch Ava's hand.

"Isn't she?" Julia said and then clamped her mouth shut. She was acting like a proud parent instead of what she was, the girlfriend of Ava's father.

Finn stood up next and stepped up beside Harper, slipping his arm around her waist and giving it a squeeze. "Someday, babe," he whispered, but it was loud enough that Julia heard.

And then came Liam, bounding up and patting Ava's head affectionately. "This is going to be a riot!" he said. When they all stared at him, he said, "What? I can't wait to see Connor as a dad."

"What about you?" Julia teased. "Don't you want to be a dad someday?"

"Gotta meet the right girl first," he said, and everyone stilled.

"Shit. Sorry, dude," Liam said to Connor.

"Forget about it," Connor said, looking down at his hands.

Julia struggled to come up with some witty comment to ease the tension but failed. Luckily, Harper stepped in.

"Julia's great with kids. I'm sure she'll be a big help to you, Connor."

"She already is," he said, shooting Julia a grateful smile.

And then the doorbell rang, puncturing the awkward moment.

"Hello? It's your mom and dad," Mrs. O'Brien called as she and her husband came in.

"Oh boy. Here we go," Liam said with a look of amusement.

The group parted, leaving Julia standing there with Ava, and she shot Connor a panicky look. He should have been the one holding his daughter, not her. But it was too late. Barbara O'Brien was already heading straight toward Julia, her arms outstretched.

"Oh my goodness! Who is this sweet little baby girl?"

Daniel O'Brien had paused and was looking around the room at his sons as if to sniff out the culprit. When his eyes landed on Connor, who was scratching the back of his neck furiously, his eyes widened with understanding.

Luckily, Ava was cooperating beautifully, garnering Barbara's full attention by smiling and cooing.

"Is she a relative of yours?" Barbara asked Julia.

"Um…no…"

Suddenly, Connor rose from his seat and walked over to where they were standing. Gently taking Ava from Julia, he held her facing outward like a shield and said, "Mom, Dad. I'd like you to meet my daughter, Ava."

All eyes shifted to Barbara, and nobody moved a muscle as they awaited her reaction.

"Your daughter? But how? When?" She looked Julia up and down as if she'd been secretly carrying Connor's baby all this time and Barbara had missed it.

Julia would have laughed had she not noticed the stricken look on Connor's face. He'd been apprehensive before, but now he looked terrified. Julia had known his family long enough to understand Barbara's role in the family. In a household full of men, she'd had to hold her own, and she was a tough lady with strong opinions that she didn't hesitate to share. Her boys were no longer under her control; however, they still revered and respected her, and nobody wanted to endure her wrath.

But Julia also knew that underneath Barbara's hard-as-nails exterior, she had a soft heart and she loved her boys tremendously even when they screwed up. Everyone knew that Barbara was itching to have grandchildren, but she'd probably never expected it to happen like this. Thus, the reason for Connor's discomfort.

"Remember Cam?" Connor said.

"The blonde woman who was a little full of herself?" Barbara said.

Liam snickered in the background until Finn punched him in the arm.

"Yes. Well, it turns out that she was pregnant when we broke up, and she neglected to tell me until now." The second the words were out, Connor looked visibly relieved.

But Barbara wasn't done. "Well, where is she? I'd like to give her a piece of my mind!"

"Barb," Daniel warned.

"I mean it. What kind of woman has a baby and doesn't tell the father?"

A blonde woman who's a little too full of herself, Julia wanted to say.

"It doesn't matter, Mom. Now that I know, I'm going to be completely involved in Ava's life."

With that, Ava gave a little cry, and Barbara immediately sprang into action.

"Poor baby. Come to Grandma," she said, whisking Ava out of Connor's arms.

"I'll warm up her bottle," Julia said, grateful for a reason to escape.

"I'll come with you," Harper said, jumping up and following her.

As soon as they were alone in the kitchen, Julia let out a breath. "Holy cow. That was intense," she said as she stuck the bottle in the microwave.

Harper eyed her with concern. "How are you handling this, Jules? I mean, you had to be shocked."

"Shocked doesn't begin to cover it."

"What did Connor have to say for himself?"

"What could he say? He was blindsided by this too. That's what he was doing in Denver a few weeks ago—meeting Ava for the first time."

Harper shook her head. "I can't imagine what that must have been like."

"I know, which is why I'm trying to keep it together—for him."

"Jules," Harper said, placing a hand on her arm. "Your feelings are important too. Don't let Connor's problems weigh you down."

"But they're my problems now too," she argued.

"Only if you want them to be," Harper said.

Ava's cries were escalating, and Julia hurriedly took the bottle out of the microwave and squirted some formula on her wrist. "This is good," she said, looking up to find Harper staring at her. "What?"

"I just hope you know what you're getting into," Harper said.

Me too.

Chapter 8

Shortly after the proud new grandma fed Ava her bottle and she'd fallen asleep, Connor kicked his family out. He'd used the excuse that Ava needed to nap, but the real reason was that he wanted to be alone with Julia. Not to mention that he'd grown tired of his family's scrutiny, especially his mother's.

He'd answered her questions the best he could and had watched Julia grow more uncomfortable with each one until he'd decided he couldn't take it anymore. So now Ava was napping in her bouncy seat where he could still see her, and he and Julia were sitting on the couch—alone.

"Can I get you anything? Are you hungry or thirsty?" he asked.

"No. I'm okay."

But he wasn't convinced. So far, she'd been amazing throughout this ordeal, but he saw the doubt and worry in her eyes, and he'd give anything to erase it.

"Are you sure? I've got chocolate."

That perked her up for a second. "What kind of chocolate?"

"Your favorite—plain Hershey bars."

"Really? When did you have time to go out and buy chocolate?"

"You'd be amazed at how good I am at multitasking," he teased, anxious to bring a smile to her face.

And it worked. "I could have some chocolate."

"Great. Stay right here," he said and disappeared into the kitchen.

Seconds later, he handed her the Hershey bar, which she promptly unwrapped and took a bite of.

"Mmm," she said. "So good."

Tugging on a strand of her hair, he said, "I'd rather hear you say that to me."

"I just did," she teased.

Watching her sitting there enjoying her candy bar, he felt a sense of peace wash over him. She was a woman of simple pleasures, and he admired that about her. She enjoyed being at home with a takeout pizza and a chocolate bar more than any other woman he'd ever known, including Cam. Cam's tastes had run to the more exotic and expensive, and looking back, he realized he'd never have been able to make her happy. But with Julia, it had been relatively easy until he'd screwed it up.

"Thanks," she said, licking the chocolate off her fingers.

He'd been watching her before, but now he openly stared and tried to tamp down his arousal. Luckily, she hadn't even noticed since she was busy licking her fingers and keeping an eye on Ava, who was still sleeping peacefully.

"You're going to be a great mom someday," he said, which made her snap her head around. *Oops. Maybe not the right thing to say.*

But she recovered quickly and said, "I hope so."

"I know so. Look how good you are with Ava. It's like you're already in tune with her."

"I love babies. It just comes natural to me."

"I wish I could say the same."

Setting the empty candy bar wrapper on the table, she placed her hand on his thigh. She'd meant it to be comforting, but he was anything but, his pants becoming tighter by the second.

"You'll get there," she said sweetly, giving his thigh a squeeze.

Connor winced, which made her look down at his lap.

"Oh!" she said, noticing the reason for his discomfort.

"Yeah. Serious discussion or not, he's got a mind of his own."

And then she gave him that full-on smile that he loved, gums showing and everything, which didn't help the situation with his pants.

"We might have some time before Ava wakes up," she said, wiggling her eyebrows at him.

"Let's hope so," he said, pulling her onto his lap.

What was it about this woman that made him want to touch her constantly? And it didn't just have to be sexually, although that was part of it. He just wanted her near him, wanted to be able to twist a lock of her hair around his finger, wanted to feel her thigh brush against his when they sat together, or having her straddle him on the couch worked too.

Threading his hands in her silky hair, he brought her face down to his and kissed her, gently at first, testing to see how far she was willing to go. When her lips parted for him, he groaned and plundered her mouth with his tongue, tasting the chocolate that still lingered there.

Adjusting herself on his lap to get closer, her breasts brushed against his chest, and he felt the hard peaks of her nipples poke into him.

If it weren't for the baby sleeping across the room, he would have already stripped her naked, but he was aware they might be interrupted at any minute. Still, he sank into the kiss, cupping her bottom in his hands and rocking into her hips.

He wasn't great at telling her how he felt, but he was damn good at showing her, and that's exactly what he intended to do. He had to prove to her that Cam meant nothing to him aside from being the mother of his child and that Julia, well…

"Connor?" Julia whispered against his lips.

"Yeah?"

"I really want this, but I think we should stop."

Not what he'd wanted to hear. Peeking around her, he saw that Ava was still resting soundly, her little mouth making a sucking motion in her sleep.

"Are you sure?" he asked, slipping his hands underneath her T-shirt and cupping her breasts.

She shook her head, and he chuckled at her indecision. From the way she'd been responding, he knew it wouldn't take long, and he hated to stop now. Pulling her bra cups down, he rasped his thumbs across her nipples and then tugged on the tight buds.

Arching her chest into his hands, she rubbed against his erection, making it almost painful for him. He loved seeing her like this, lost in ecstasy, void of inhibitions, and knowing that it was all because of him.

"It's okay, Julia. Just let go," he mumbled against her lips.

And she did. Right there on the couch, fully dressed, using the friction generated from their clothed bodies to come undone. Connor thought it might be one of the most erotic moments they'd shared yet, and there had been quite a few.

Wrapping his arms around her waist, he held her tight as she came back to herself, her head resting on his shoulder. When they were together like this, he felt like there wasn't anything they couldn't overcome. Not her family's disapproval, not her doctor ex-boyfriend who was still lurking in the background, and not Cam, who had come back into his life unexpectedly.

Stroking her back, he felt extremely lucky that she was still there. Some other woman might have cut and run at the first sign of trouble, but not her. She was tougher than she looked, stronger than she believed, and more important to him than she knew.

He vowed to change that, but he wouldn't rush it because, right now, they still had a lot to deal with, and the situation with Ava was still new.

"What about you?" Julia whispered, her breath skimming over his neck and making him squirm.

"What about me?"

"You know," she said, motioning to his lap.

But just then, Ava let out a peep, and they both stilled.

"Maybe she'll go back to sleep," he said, but he doubted it. He was already learning how unpredictable babies could be. As if to prove it, Ava let out a squeal, letting them know she was truly awake.

"I owe you one," Julia said as she crawled off his lap and walked across the room.

She reached Ava before he'd even gotten up, and carefully lifted her out of the bouncy seat.

Damn, they make a pretty picture, he thought as Julia walked toward him.

"Here's your daddy," Julia said, handing Ava off to him.

All his worries were forgotten as he folded his beautiful daughter into his embrace. But when he glanced up at Julia, she was gazing at them wistfully.

Well, not all my worries.

Chapter 9

The next day, Julia pulled into the parking lot of her dad's pediatric practice. Parking next to his blue Mercedes, she sighed. As the only child, it had been expected that she would follow in her father's footsteps and become a doctor or a nurse, but the mere sight of a needle made her squeamish. Much to her father's chagrin, she'd decided to study accounting, a much neater profession without all that messy human emotion attached to it. Give her a spreadsheet full of figures, and she was happy.

After obtaining her accounting degree, Julia had reluctantly agreed to begin her career by taking over the accounting tasks at her father's office. Call it familial duty or, more accurately, guilt. But three years later, when she'd seen the ad in the paper for an accountant at a nearby photography studio, she'd jumped at the chance.

When she'd first told her parents about wanting to quit, they'd been so disappointed that she'd offered to continue working for them on the side. But she'd made it very clear that her first priority was her job with Harper. So far, she'd been able to juggle both jobs and keep both of her employers happy.

Before she and Connor had started dating, she would have looked forward to going there, but not today. She hadn't spoken much to her parents since the night she and Connor had had dinner with them. It was difficult knowing that her parents were disappointed in her, but she was a grown woman, and she could make her own decisions about who to date.

She suspected that their disappointment had less to do with Connor and more to do with her breakup with Alec. After all, it was her father who had set her up with Alec in the first place. As the son of one of her dad's colleagues, their families had always been close. At first, Alec had seemed like the perfect match for her as they had a lot in common, including their Asian-American heritage.

But after dating for almost a year, they'd started discussing marriage, and it was then that their relationship had fallen apart. She still remembered the conversation very clearly…

"If we're going to get married, we should probably discuss some of the big issues that can cause problems, don't you think?" she'd asked him over dinner one night.

"Like what?" Alec said as he used a fork and spoon to twist some spaghetti noodles into a perfect bite-sized portion. He was nothing if not meticulous.

"You know, like money for example. Who's going to balance the checkbook? Are we going to have a joint account or keep separate funds? That sort of thing."

Alec swallowed his bite and dabbed the corners of his mouth with a napkin. He was the only person she knew who could eat spaghetti without getting a drop of sauce on him. Thinking of that, Julia glanced down at her blouse and discovered that yes, indeed, there was a bright orange stain right above her left breast. Dipping a napkin in her water glass, she dabbed at the stain and waited for Alec to respond.

But instead of answering her questions, he said, "That's just going to make it worse. Why don't you wait until you get home to treat the stain?" And then he looked around the restaurant as if to make sure that nobody was watching them.

While she usually admired his affinity for neatness, sometimes it really bugged the crap out of her—like now. Who cared if she was wiping a stain off her boob? Nobody was paying them the least bit of attention.

"You haven't answered my questions," she said, giving up on the stain.

"Well, I think it's pretty obvious. You're the one with the accounting degree, so you should balance the checkbook. And I don't see any reason to have separate accounts. What's mine is yours, and vice versa." With that, he went back to his spaghetti.

"So, that's it? Just because I'm an accountant, I have to balance the checkbook?" She wasn't sure why that bothered her, but it did. Maybe it was because of the haughty way he'd said it, almost like he couldn't be bothered with such a menial task.

Alec didn't flinch. He simply swallowed his bite and then set down his fork again before answering. "Would you rather mow the lawn instead?"

"Huh?" She wasn't sure what the correlation was, but he was about to explain.

"The way I see it, I'll probably be the one who mows the lawn and takes care of the outside maintenance because that's what guys do. I wouldn't ask you to do it because it doesn't seem like something you'd be interested in. Just like I'm not particularly interested in balancing the checkbook. See? It all works out in the end."

But Julia wasn't done. "What if I *want* to mow the lawn? Are you not going to let me?"

She must have ruffled him, because his brow quirked up a notch on the right side. It wasn't much, but it was a sign that she'd gotten to him. Why she felt victorious over that, she had no idea.

"Do you *want* to mow the lawn?" he asked incredulously.

"Not particularly, but that's beside the point. If I did want to, I should be able to."

"Fine. If you want to mow the lawn, go ahead, but I'm still not interested in balancing the checkbook."

Just then, the waitress came over and asked if they wanted dessert.

"Yes," Julia said.

"No," Alec said simultaneously.

The waitress looked between them and giggled, but neither of them joined in her laughter.

This was another glitch in their relationship. Julia loved chocolate and desserts in general; however, Alec was a strict eater who only indulged in dessert on special occasions. No amount of coaxing would get him to change his mind. She'd tried everything, including using dessert to lure him into the bedroom, but the man wouldn't budge. She didn't like to think about what that said about their sex life.

After a while, Julia had stopped trying, but she didn't let that prevent her from ordering dessert. "I'll have a hot fudge brownie with whipped cream and a cherry on top," she said proudly.

Alec remained silent until the waitress walked away, and then he leaned across the table and said, "You know how bad all that sugar is for you, right?"

The joys of dating a doctor-in-training. Having a father who was a doctor, you'd have thought she'd be used to it, but compared to Alec, her dad was lenient. Instead of preaching abstinence (with food), he talked about maintaining a balanced diet, and that included occasional treats.

So, growing up, Julia had learned to enjoy her dessert in small quantities. Tonight, however, she planned to eat the entire hot fudge brownie just out of spite.

Ignoring the sugar comment, she said, "Let's move on to another topic, shall we?"

"Sure. Which topic do you want to discuss next?"

"Kids," she said without hesitation.

This time, his jaw twitched, and she wondered what it meant. Since he hadn't said anything yet, she continued. "I'd like to have at least two or three, God willing."

Alec picked up his water glass and took a long drink, averting his eyes the entire time.

Uh-oh. This doesn't look promising.

"Well?" she asked when he'd finished drinking.

Clearing his throat, Alec said, "I'm not really interested in having children."

BOOM! Julia's jaw dropped, her eyes bugged out, and she accidentally leaned forward, right into her plate of spaghetti. And the kicker was, he'd said it as matter-of-factly as he'd said he wasn't interested in balancing the checkbook. Hello? Two completely different things!

"You're…not…*interested*?" she stammered.

And there came the waitress, bearing a plate piled high with a mammoth brownie, vanilla ice cream, hot fudge, whipped cream, and a cherry on top. The waitress took one look at Julia's soiled blouse and said, "Oh. I'm so sorry about your top. I should have cleared your plate earlier, but I didn't think you were done."

"Oh, we're *done*," Julia said, looking at Alec pointedly.

But true to his character, he didn't dare show a flicker of emotion in front of the waitress. Had the man always been this stoic? How had she not noticed?

The waitress hurriedly cleared their plates, and then she set the dessert in front of Julia. "It's on the house," she said before walking away.

The dessert looked and smelled wonderful, but Julia wanted to wrap up their conversation first.

"Do you mean you're not interested in having two or three? Because I guess we could compromise on that," she said.

Alec shook his head. "No. That's not what I meant. I meant that I don't want to have any."

"Any as in none? Zero? Zilch?"

"That's right," he said.

She honestly couldn't believe it. Not just that he didn't want kids but that they'd never discussed this before. How could they not have? She loved kids. Her dad was a pediatrician, for God's sake. She'd known she'd wanted children since she was a child herself. How could this be happening?

"I can see that you're upset by this," Alec said, interrupting her thoughts. "But it doesn't mean we can't work something out."

Eyebrows raised, she said, "How? You don't want kids, and I do. How do we work that out?" She hadn't realized how loud she was being until she noticed the lady at the table next to them staring.

Lowering his voice, Alec said, "Aren't you going to eat that?"

Glancing down at her plate, Julia saw that her beautiful dessert was turning into a pile of mush, and it suddenly looked very unappetizing. It would be one of the very few times in her life she'd turn away dessert.

"No. I'm not interested," she said and stood up abruptly.

"Julia. Wait. Where are you going?"

"Home."

"You can't leave without me. I drove," he said, a touch of panic in his voice.

"Hand me your keys."

"Why?"

"Hand me your keys," she repeated, eyes narrowing at him.

This time, he must have realized that she was serious, because he fished his keys out of his pocket and placed them in her hand. She'd turned to walk away when he said, "How am I supposed to get home?"

"You're going to be a doctor. You figure it out," she said and stomped off to the sound of the lady clapping from the next table over.

After she and Alec had broken up, she hadn't minded working the extra hours, but now that Connor was in the picture, and Ava too, she would have rather been with them. *Them.* How funny, that she was already thinking of them as a set when a week ago it had just been him. And then she realized that she hadn't told her parents about Ava yet. If they were already displeased about her dating Connor, how would they feel once they found out he had a child?

She was so lost in thought that she forgot she was sitting in her car until another vehicle pulled up and parked in the space beside her. When she glanced over, she said, "Oh no. Not again."

They stepped out of their cars at the same time, and Alec said, "Hey, Jules."

"What are you doing here?" she snapped even though she already knew the answer.

"I'm meeting with Dr. Lee to go over some questions I have."

Ugh. How was it that she'd managed to avoid him for months and now he kept showing up just like a bad penny. *As if I don't have enough to deal with.*

Turning away, she started walking toward the front door, and in two long strides, Alec was right beside her.

"Are you working today?" he asked.

It was obvious he was trying to make small talk, but she really wasn't up to it.

"Yes, but if I'd have known you would be here…"

"You wouldn't have come. Yeah. I kind of gathered that."

"Look, Alec. I don't mean to be rude, but it's a little awkward, don't you think?"

"What is?"

"You hanging out with my dad. Us running into each other. When people break up, they're not meant to keep in contact. That's kind of the whole idea behind breaking up."

Alec smiled at her, not looking the least bit offended. "I see you still have that quirky sense of humor."

Ignoring him, she slid her key in the lock, opened the door, and stepped inside with him right on her heels. Hearing her dad's voice, she figured he was on the phone, and she was just as glad. She wasn't ready to face him yet, and now she had Alec to deal with too.

"I wasn't kidding, Alec. It was kind of upsetting when you showed up at Mom and Dad's house the night I was there with Connor."

"Connor, huh. So, you're still seeing him?"

"Yes," she said as she went behind the front desk and set down her purse. She hoped Alec would take the hint that she didn't want to talk when she turned her back and started digging through a file drawer for some papers she needed.

"How's that working out?" he asked. Once again, she wondered how he was able to stay so cool and detached. Was he missing the part of the brain that processed emotions? Did he want to be friends now? Or was he just trying to be nice because of her dad?

"It's going good," she said, but she must not have sounded convincing enough.

"You sure?"

"Yes. Why do you ask?"

"I just care about you, that's all. Even though things didn't work out for us, I still want you to be happy."

Setting down the file folder she'd been holding, she looked him in the eyes for the first time in a long time. She searched for a trace of insincerity, jealousy, or ulterior motives, but she came up empty. *Empty.* That was a good word for how she felt about Alec now. It was hard to believe that at one time, she'd wanted to marry him. It was amazing how much had changed in the course of a few months, weeks, or days (in the case of Ava's arrival). Julia felt like a different person now, a better version of herself. And if Alec was being this civil toward her, she owed him the same courtesy.

"What about you? Are you dating anyone new?"

"No. I'm too busy with my studies to think about dating," he said.

Just then, Dr. Lee walked up behind Alec and clapped him on the shoulder.

Her father walked so softly that she hadn't heard him approach, and she wondered how much he'd overheard.

He shook Alec's hand and then turned to her. "Good morning, sweetheart. I wasn't sure if you'd be here today."

"It's my Sunday to work," she replied, shooting him a tentative smile. She hated the awkwardness between them, but she wasn't sure how to smooth things over. If her parents had reservations about Connor before, wait until they found out about Cam and Ava.

"Well, I'm glad you're here. Maybe we can have lunch together when you're done working, and Alec can join us."

And just like that, she shut down again.

"Thanks for the invite, Dr. Lee, but I have plans this afternoon," Alec said unexpectedly.

"So do I," Julia said. Part of her hated to turn her dad down, but once he'd invited Alec along, she'd realized what was up to. Her dad was still trying to push her and Alec back together, but it wasn't going to work, and the sooner he realized that, the better.

"Some other time, then," Dr. Lee said, and then turning to Alec, he said, "We can talk in my office."

Julia watched her father and Alec walk away, but right before Alec went into her dad's office, he looked over his shoulder and gave her an apologetic look. She'd wondered if he had conspired with her parents to win her back, but now she doubted it. She should have felt relieved, but she didn't. She still had to address the issues she had with her parents, and she still had to tell them about Ava.

Since when did my life become so complicated? Oh, right. Since I started dating Connor O'Brien.

Chapter 10

"Good news," Connor said when he called her the next day.

"What is?"

"Cam's agreed to stay in Michigan."

Julia and Harper were in the photo studio, and Harper shot her a curious glance. It was hard to label Connor's news as "good" when it meant that his attractive ex-girlfriend, the woman who'd birthed his baby, was going to be living nearby.

"That is good news, I guess," Julia said.

"This means that I'll get to see Ava as often as I want, which is a helluva lot better than traveling back and forth to Colorado, don't you think?"

We'll see. "Yes. I'm happy for you," she said, angling her body away from Harper's intense stare.

"The next step is to find them someplace to live," he said almost as if he were talking to himself.

"Harper knows a real estate agent who could help with that," Julia suggested. *Okay, how did I just go from feeling jealous to wanting to help?*

Harper's eyes were practically popping out of her head now. It was impossible to have a private conversation in the tiny studio, but they were best

102

friends, and since Harper was already familiar with the situation, Julia didn't feel like she had anything to hide.

"Cam can't afford a house right now. She wants to look for an apartment, and she asked me to help her."

"Of course she did," Julia said. Trying to keep the ugly green monster from creeping up on her was impossible, but she vowed to try harder. It certainly wouldn't help anything for Connor to know how jealous she was.

"She doesn't have a lot of friends, Jules, and her parents aren't in good health. She needs my help."

"What about her boyfriend—the boss?"

"They're not seeing each other anymore, at least not personally."

How could he believe her after all the lies? First, she'd had an affair with a married man, and then she'd kept Ava from him for five months.

"And you believe her?" Julia said, realizing how bitter she sounded. But she couldn't help it. She understood him wanting to spend as much time with his daughter as possible, but she hated that Cam was worming her way back into his life too. Julia wasn't convinced that all Cam wanted was his help.

"I believe that she wants what's best for Ava," he said solemnly.

Realizing that she had no choice in the matter, Julia said, "If you need to help Cam find an apartment, then I'll have to accept that. But I don't have to like it."

Connor laughed, and it helped ease the tension between them.

"You could come with us," he said.

"Not a chance."

He laughed again.

"When are you going?" she asked.

"Tonight, after work."

"Oh. Are you taking Ava too?"

"I was thinking about asking my mom to babysit so we don't have to lug her in and out of the car."

"I'll babysit." *Whoa! What is wrong with me? I'm aiding and abetting the enemy.*

Connor was silent for a few seconds, as if giving her time to retract her offer.

"I mean, it's no problem, and then you and I will get to see each other too. It's kind of a win-win."

"Are you sure? Because I know my mom would be thrilled to take her."

"Connor. If you and are going to be together, then I have to accept that Ava's part of your life too. It'll be good for me to bond with her. Besides, I'm great with babies. How hard can it be?"

"Shhh. Don't cry, sweetheart. It's okay."

Julia paced back and forth across Connor's living room floor, wearing a path in the carpet. She'd come over right after work to watch Ava while he and Cam went apartment hunting. When they'd left, Ava had been contentedly shoving her fist in her mouth, showing no signs of distress. But an hour later, Julia couldn't get her to stop crying.

She'd tried everything—feeding her, changing her, and burping her—but nothing seemed to help. She'd even broken into song, calling upon some of her favorite childhood tunes, but either her voice was off key or this baby was extremely stubborn, because she still hadn't settled down.

Julia racked her brain for ideas she'd heard from her friends who had kids, but they seemed either too far-fetched or impossible (in the case of putting Ava to her breast and letting her suckle).

She'd even considered taking Ava for a car ride, but when she'd examined the car seat that Cam had left with all its hooks and straps, she'd gotten nervous. She couldn't in good conscience take Ava for a drive if she wasn't sure how to install the car seat. It shouldn't be rocket science, but she wasn't taking any chances with somebody else's baby.

And there it was again. The reminder slapped her in the face and took her breath away. *If she were my baby, I'd probably know exactly what to do. But she's not.*

Just then, as if Ava had decided to give Julia a break, she stopped crying. Just like that. Julia was so excited that she lifted Ava overhead and gave her a huge smile. "Thank you," she said, and instead of a "You're welcome," she got a face full of drool, but she was too happy to care.

When Connor and Cam returned a while later, Ava was resting peacefully in Julia's arms.

"Wow. Look at you," Connor said as he came into the room. "Cam said Ava was kind of fussy today, but you'd never know it now."

"Really? She wasn't fussy for me at all," Julia said, looking Cam straight in the face. *Okay. That was a low blow, but it's not fair that Cam got to spend the last three hours with my boyfriend!*

"How did the apartment hunting go?" Julia asked as Cam began collecting Ava's belongings and stuffing them in the diaper bag.

"I haven't made up my mind yet. I think Connor and I are going to look again over the weekend when we have more time," Cam said. She'd put everything away and stood in front of Julia with her hands on her narrow hips as if daring her to argue.

Looking between them with a pinched expression, Connor said to Julia, "I said I'd check with you first and work it around our plans."

Julia was touched that he'd stepped up for them, and she wanted to kiss him. However, she was still holding a sleeping baby, so she settled for shooting him a wide smile instead.

"I should get Ava home," Cam said, bending over to take her from Julia. That made the second time Julia had seen down her shirt.

Has she ever heard of a camisole? Julia wondered.

"I'll walk you out," Connor said, bringing the car seat over so Cam could strap Ava into it.

"I'll come too," Julia said, ignoring the scowl on Cam's face. "I'd like to see how this thing works."

Cam couldn't very well argue when it came to the safety of her baby. So, the three of them went outside: Connor carrying Ava in the car seat, Cam carrying the diaper bag, and Julia sporting a satisfied smile. If Cam thought she was going to get more alone time with Connor, she had another think coming!

As Cam was showing Connor how to install the car seat, Julia fought back the urge to laugh. The situation was comical if one bothered to find the humor in it. It was like a joke—How many people does it take to strap in a car seat? Three: the mom, the dad, and the jealous girlfriend! She doubted that Cam would find it funny, but Julia squirreled it away for later when she could tell Harper.

Once Ava was properly strapped in, having slept through the whole ordeal, they said their goodbyes. And if Julia had thought she was preventing something from happening by coming outside with them, she'd been wrong. Before she knew it, Cam had thrown her arms around Connor's neck and hugged him, pressing her tiny breasts against his broad chest.

"Thank you so much for coming with me tonight," she said, gazing at him as if Julia weren't even there.

When she pulled back, Connor had that deer-in-the-headlights look, and shoving his hands in his front pockets, he said, "You're welcome."

With that, Cam trotted her slim little booty around to the driver's side of the car and slid in, not bothering to say goodbye to Julia or thanking her for watching Ava. *That little b—*

Once Connor had herded Julia back into the house and shut the door, he scooped her up into his arms and started walking down the hall toward his bedroom. He sat down on the edge of his bed with her on his lap and gently tucked a strand of hair behind her ear.

"You're the one she should have thanked," he said with an apologetic look on his handsome face.

"Doesn't matter. I did it for you, not her."

"Then allow me to properly thank you."

And with that, he tipped her back on the bed and captured her lips in a searing kiss.

When he pulled back, she said, "That's a good start, but you'll have to do better. Ava was *really* fussy tonight."

Connor gaped at her. "I thought you said she was good."

Julia shrugged. "I was being spiteful, and I'm not sorry about it."

Laughing, he stroked a finger over her bottom lip. "I love that about you."

"You do?"

"Um-hmm. I love that you are who you are and you don't make any apologies for it."

"Thanks, I guess."

"I'm the one who's supposed to be thanking you, remember?"

Skimming his hand down her side, he slipped it under her shirt and drew tantalizing patterns on her skin with his fingertip.

It would have been so easy to close off her mind and surrender; however, she still felt conflicted about Cam. And since he'd said that he admired her honesty (not in those exact words, but still), she decided to capitalize on it.

"I know what you said about Cam wanting what's best for Ava, but don't you think she might have her own interests in mind too?"

"Such as?"

He seemed distracted as his hand drifted further up her shirt.

"You."

His hand stilled, and he stared down at her with a bewildered expression.

"Oh, come on. That cocky guy I first met wouldn't look so surprised," she said.

"That was your description, not mine."

"So, you don't think she has any interest in you whatsoever?"

He shook his head. "No. I don't. What we had was over a long time ago."

"That's the same for me and Alec, yet you seem to think he's still interested in me."

"That's because he is."

"How do you know?"

"I just do."

She wanted to argue that she felt the same way about Cam but decided not to. Instead of harping on the subject with him, maybe it'd be better to go straight to the source. A woman-to-woman talk. That's what she needed to put her mind at ease. Feeling better now that she'd set a course of action, Julia took Connor's right hand and placed it on her breast.

"We done talking?" he asked, giving it a squeeze.

"I have just one more thing to say." And after tormenting him with a dramatic pause, she said, "Undress me."

Chapter 11

"My pleasure," Connor said, and then he unwrapped her like a long-awaited-for gift on Christmas morning. As often as they'd done this, he was still blown away by her beauty. The way her silky black hair fanned out over the pillow. How her eyelids became hooded as he caressed her skin. How responsive she was to every touch, every kiss, every lick.

He needed this. Needed her more every day.

Once he'd removed her clothes, he slid off the bed and gazed at her for a long moment, his eyes sweeping down the length of her curvy body and back up again. He liked doing this—soaking her up with his eyes before they made love.

Squirming beneath his gaze, her nipples tightened, and she clamped her legs together as if to shield herself.

"Don't hide from me, Jules. Let me see you."

"You do see me," she said, her shaky voice another indicator of her arousal.

"All of you," he said.

She seemed to be warring with herself until she slowly spread her legs apart.

Drawing in a ragged breath, Connor said, "So damn beautiful."

And then she shot him that smile, the one she reserved just for him for when they were together like this.

"Hurry up," she said.

That was all the invitation he needed, and he made quick work of shedding his clothes. They hadn't had sex in several days other than when she'd climaxed with her clothes on the other day, and he was rock hard from wanting her.

He'd meant to treat her to a slow and steady buildup, but at this rate, he wasn't going to last long. And then he saw a movement out of the corner of his eye and realized that she'd already gotten started without him.

It was the sexiest thing he'd ever seen, and his desire skyrocketed.

He stood there, frozen to the spot, and watched her pleasure herself, the blood pounding in his head. Hell, he probably could have stood there all night if it weren't for his throbbing erection.

Damn this woman! She constantly surprised him.

"Connor…" she panted, pleading with her eyes.

"Sorry." At her urging, he quickly retrieved a condom from his dresser drawer and rolled it on while she continued to play.

As he crawled over her, he almost hated to interrupt. But when she removed her hand and gripped his hips instead, he was instantly glad he did.

Guiding himself inside her slippery entrance, he groaned with pleasure. Then, lowering his mouth to hers, he tangled with her tongue, and the combination was too much. The sexy little peep show she'd given him had him plummeting over the edge after a few hearty thrusts.

He might have felt bad about it if she hadn't followed him over just as enthusiastically, clinging to his back and strangling his waist with her legs.

Sweaty and sated, he rolled off her and flopped onto his back, his chest heaving.

Leaning her head on his shoulder, Julia said, "You okay?"

"Just a little lightheaded," he teased, although it wasn't far from the truth. The visual of her hand between her legs was still stuck in his head, and it wasn't something he'd soon forget. When he glanced down to see her self-satisfied smile, he suspected she knew as much—the little vixen!

Grazing her hand over his chest, she said, "I've never done that before."

Eyes popping, he said, "You could have fooled me."

"I meant with someone watching."

"Oh." The thought of him being the only one to witness such a sight made his chest puff up, and slinging an arm around her, he pulled her closer. "Well, in case you didn't notice, I thoroughly enjoyed the show."

Giggling, she said, "I noticed."

"In fact, I'd be glad to attend a repeat performance sometime," he teased.

Instead of responding, she flung a leg over him and snuggled closer. He needed to clean up, but he hated the thought of leaving her for even two seconds.

What's wrong with me? Since when do I go this ga-ga over a woman? But he'd never known a woman like Julia before—someone so sweet and sexy at the same time. Someone who called him out on his shit and forced him to own up to his mistakes. Someone who lit up the room whenever she walked in, along with the dark corners of his heart. He hadn't been this serious about a woman—well, since Cam. But that was nothing compared to this.

His breathing had evened out, and Julia's had too. Glancing down, he saw her eyes were closed, and she appeared to be sleeping. It tugged on his heartstrings to see her looking so peaceful and content in his arms. He shook his head, thinking again that he didn't deserve her and wondering why she put up with a guy like him. Especially now, with everything that had happened.

Slowly withdrawing from the bed, he left to clean up, but first, he covered her with the sheet. As much as he loved to look at her naked body, he didn't want her to get cold. Go figure. Finding out that he was a father was turning him into a sensitive guy. He'd gone from only worrying about himself to caring for not one but two girls—Julia and Ava.

After he'd cleaned himself off, he leaned over the bathroom sink and examined himself in the mirror. His hair was tousled from where Julia had scraped her hands through it. His stubble had popped out, and he wondered if he'd left marks on her skin. And then he twisted his body around and looked over his shoulder at his back, where he saw indentions from her fingernails. The thought of it made him smile, but then he quickly sobered.

This woman had freely given him her body, but each time they were together, she was giving him her heart too. He saw it in her eyes, in the way she said his name, in the way she touched him. And while he was starting to feel the same way, it scared him because he knew the risks involved.

He'd opened his heart before, and look what had happened. The one woman he thought he'd loved had cheated on him. After that, he'd guarded his heart carefully, unwilling to let someone else in. It had been easier that way. Better to have a short-term fling and be the one to walk away rather than let someone else stomp all over him. He was fine as long as he was in control. Or so he'd thought before Julia.

When they'd first met, he'd wanted to put her in the same category as the other women he'd been with since Cam. And even though he suspected she wasn't that type of woman, she'd agreed. But it hadn't taken long before he'd found himself wanting to spend more time with her, wanting to get to know her better. With each passing day, he found himself caring more about her, and that included wanting to protect her. But protect her from what—him?

It brought a smile to his face thinking how she didn't want to be protected. She was braver and stronger than him when it came to matters of the heart. Hadn't she proven that by the way she'd stood by him through this mess with Cam?

He knew it couldn't be easy, Julia seeing his exgirlfriend waltz back into his life with his baby. He'd seen the flickers of jealousy on her face, and she'd all but admitted it a few times. It pained him that she felt threatened by Cam even after he'd told her she had nothing to worry about. But how could he convince her of that? His word alone didn't seem to be doing the trick, and who could blame her? They hadn't even been together that long, and he didn't exactly have a stellar reputation when it came to relationships. She was smart to be wary.

But he hated seeing the uncertainty on her face whenever Cam was around. He'd give anything to erase her doubt. But how?

Chapter 12

The day had started out perfectly. It was one of those gorgeous spring days in May where the sun is bright but the temperature is a comfortable seventy degrees. It was perfect weather for eating dinner outside on the patio of her favorite restaurant with Connor and their friends. It had been his idea, and Julia had jumped on it.

So, there they all were, she and Connor, Harper and Finn, and Julia's cousin Will and his fiancée, Megan. They'd also invited Liam, the youngest O'Brien brother, and Harper's sister, McKayla, but neither of them had shown up yet.

There were two pitchers of beer on the table and several appetizers, and as the breeze gently ruffled her hair, Julia scooted her chair a little closer to Connor.

She'd worn a dress for the occasion, and Connor rested his hand on her bare knee beneath the table while they conversed with their friends.

"So, have you two set a date yet?" Harper asked Will.

Initially, Julia had tried setting Harper up with Will, but they'd turned out to be better off as friends, and now he was engaged to Megan. Julia noticed that

Finn had casually draped his arm over Harper's shoulder, and she smiled. *Everyone is with the right person*, she thought while observing the two couples.

"Not yet," Will said.

"But we're getting closer," Megan said.

"What's the holdup?" Julia asked.

"We're trying to figure out the best place to get married since Megan's family is scattered across the country," Will said.

"Oh. So, there might be a destination wedding?" Harper said excitedly.

"Could be," Will replied, smiling sweetly at his fiancée.

"Well, the sooner you let everyone know, the better," Julia said. "No pressure or anything."

Everyone laughed.

Julia noticed that Connor and Finn had been particularly quiet during the exchange, but she didn't think much of it. Women were always more interested in weddings than men anyway.

Just then, Finn flagged down their waitress and asked for another pitcher of beer since he and Connor had finished the one sitting between them.

Speaking of weddings, Julia wondered when Finn might pop the question to Harper. The two of them had moved in together, and she expected that they'd get engaged sometime soon. Harper had put her house up for sale with her real estate friend, Nicole Collins. She'd had several showings, but nobody had made an offer yet. *Maybe Finn's waiting for Harper's house to sell before he proposes*, Julia mused.

And then she realized that all her closest friends were either married, engaged, or having babies. Everyone except her. She wanted all those things too, but given the current situation, she wondered when or if it would happen for her. She had started to envision a future with Connor, but that was before Cam and Ava had shown up. Now her vision was muddled. It was challenging enough to have a relationship between two people, let alone four!

Shaking her head, she tried to rejoin the conversation about Will's wedding, but just then, Connor's phone beeped.

Taking it out of his pocket, he looked down at the screen and then quickly typed something before returning the phone to his pocket.

"Anything important?" Julia asked.

"That was Cam. Ava's running a fever, and she wanted to let me know."

"Oh. Poor baby. I hope she's okay."

"Yeah, me too."

After their exchange, Will nudged Megan and said, "Go ahead and ask her."

"Ask me what?" Julia said.

"We'd like you to stand up in our wedding—as one of my bridesmaids," Megan said, her expression hopeful.

"Oh," Julia replied, the request catching her off guard.

"I don't have any sisters, and my best friend is my maid of honor, but I could use another bridesmaid," Megan explained.

"I'd love to," Julia said, smiling at them. This would be the third wedding she'd stood up in recently, and she was starting to wonder if there was such a thing as a professional bridesmaid. But she loved Will like a brother, and she really liked Megan, so of course, she said yes.

"Great! I promise not to make you wear a dress that looks like an ice cream flavor," Megan said, earning a round of laughter from the group. "In fact, we can go shopping together, and you can pick out the dress."

At least there's that. "Sounds good," Julia said before taking a long swallow of beer.

As she was setting down her glass, Connor's phone buzzed again. This time, everybody stopped talking to hear the latest news.

After he read the text, he looked up to see everybody staring at him and said, "She's taking Ava to the emergency clinic."

"Babies get fevers all the time. I'm sure it's nothing," Finn said.

"Since when are you an expert on babies?" Connor said.

Connor and Finn had a volatile relationship. They could either be the best of friends or mortal enemies depending on their moods.

"Hey, I was just trying to make you feel better," Finn retorted.

"Well, don't," Connor said, stuffing the phone back in his pocket.

Placing her hand on his forearm, Julia said, "Do you want us to leave and meet Cam at the clinic?"

Glancing around the table, he shook his head. "No reason for both of us to go. Why don't you stay here, and I'll go?"

She started to argue, but then Harper piped up and said, "We can give you a ride home, Jules."

"Yeah. That's no problem," Finn affirmed.

Julia was torn between wanting to enjoy the evening with her friends and wanting to be by

Connor's side. She'd hate it if something was seriously wrong with Ava and she wasn't there. But Connor had already stood up and pushed in his chair.

"Thanks, guys. I better get going."

"I'll walk you out," Julia said before standing up and following him out to the parking lot.

"Finn's right, you know?"

"About what?" he said briskly.

"Having a fever doesn't mean it's something serious."

"Are you a doctor now too?" he said.

Up until then, she'd blamed his abruptness on his being worried about Ava, but now her patience was running out. They'd reached his Jeep, and as he went to open the door, she put her hand on his arm again.

"No, but my dad is, and I've been around a lot of sick babies. But you know what, never mind. You're obviously not interested in hearing anything I have to say."

"Shit. I'm sorry, Jules. I'm just not used to this, ya know? I don't usually get calls about a sick kid who's mine."

While she felt bad for him, she was still smarting from the way he'd treated her and his brother. "Just go. Ava needs you."

Nodding, he hopped up in the Jeep and drove away, leaving her standing there in the parking lot. He wasn't the only one who wasn't used to getting interrupted in the middle of dinner. She'd been looking forward to a relaxing night out all week long, and now it was down to her and two couples. Inhaling deeply, she plastered on a smile and went to rejoin her friends. Even with Connor gone, she was determined to enjoy the rest of the evening without him.

While Finn and Harper were driving her home, Julia checked her phone for the umpteenth time. She hadn't asked Connor to update her about Ava's condition, but she'd assumed that he would.

"This must be hard on you too," Harper said when she saw Julia looking at her phone.

Finn was driving, and he kept his eyes glued to the road, pretending not to hear.

"Yeah. It is," Julia said. "I hope Ava's okay."

"I'm sure he'll call you after he leaves the clinic," Harper said, but Julia wasn't so sure. He'd probably be too busy attending to his sick baby and consoling her mother. Once again, Julia questioned Cam's motives. Cam must know that he'd feel responsible for her and Ava and would jump in to help whenever he could. Was she using that to her advantage?

It was late by the time Finn dropped her off, and Julia still hadn't heard from Connor. She didn't feel right going to bed without knowing Ava's condition, so she decided to send him a text. She figured it would be less disruptive than a phone call, and Connor could answer her discreetly.

So, she typed: *Are you still at the clinic? How's Ava?*

When there was no reply, Julia started to get ready for bed. She hung up her dress, washed off her makeup, and put on some pajamas. Originally, she'd thought that she and Connor might spend the night together, so she'd worn a sexy bra and panty set under her dress. *There went that idea*, she thought as she tossed them into the hamper.

Connor wasn't the only one who'd have to get used to being interrupted. She'd just crawled under the sheets when her phone buzzed with an incoming text.

Connor had written: *We're home now. Ava was given an antibiotic and she's sleeping comfortably.*

Wait a minute. *We're* home now. What exactly did that mean? Julia read the text again, confused by his choice of words. Did he mean that they were each at their individual homes or that they were together? Suddenly, a chill crawled up her spine, and her nerve endings tingled with dread. *What should I do? Should I ask him if they're together? Would he tell me the truth if they were?*

But before she could make up her mind, her phone beeped again.

Cam's staying over tonight so we can both keep an eye on Ava.

And there was her answer. Her instinct had been correct—again. She'd learned to listen to her inner voice whenever something felt off, but in this case, the voice was more like a scream. Shoving off the covers, she got out of bed and started pacing.

"Am I just supposed to accept this? My boyfriend and his ex-girlfriend are staying overnight together, and I'm just supposed to sit back and let it happen?"

Her phone buzzed again, probably because she hadn't texted him back.

Jules? Are you still there?

She stared at the screen for a moment, debating how to respond, and then she typed: *I'm glad Ava's feeling better.* That was all she could manage before she shut off the phone and set it face down on her bedside table. And then she paced some more, knowing there was no way she'd get to sleep anytime soon.

She hated the idea of Cam sleeping under Connor's roof, with or without Ava there. She could just imagine what Cam wore to bed, probably something skimpy that accentuated her long, toned legs and perky little breasts. She was probably trotting around his house like that right now, or worse, they were sitting in the living room together having a nightcap.

A nightcap? Really, Jules? But still! Ava was probably sleeping soundly in the spare room, which left the two of them all alone. As she was pacing, Julia caught a glimpse of herself in the dresser mirror. Her hair was in disarray from shoving her hands through it, her face was pale and drawn, and her Hello Kitty pajama set, which she'd thought was so cute when she'd bought it, made her look like a rumpled little kid.

Damn that Cam! She with the flowy blonde hair and bright blue eyes, looking more like a runway model than a woman who'd just had a baby. Cam was really a devil in disguise, and Connor refused to see it. He'd made excuses for Cam's behavior and insisted that she only had Ava's best interest in mind. But how could he trust her? And could Julia trust him? After all, he didn't owe her anything. They were dating, but that wasn't the same as having a true commitment to one another. They hadn't even exchanged words of love, which would have been something to hang on to, but there wasn't even that. What did they share other than a heart-pounding physical attraction and some mutual friends, two things that would be easy to walk away from?

Finally, tired of pacing, Julia slipped back into bed. She picked up her phone, and sure enough, Connor had tried to call, but he hadn't left a message or sent any more texts. He'd probably given up on her and was currently being seduced by the blonde she-devil. Setting her phone down, Julia turned her back on it and curled into herself.

"Fine. You can have him!" she shouted. But a few minutes later, once she'd started to settle down, she realized that it wasn't fine at all. *Nothing* about this situation was fine. And the question that nagged at her as she tried to sleep was: *What am I going to do about it?*

Chapter 13

Julia rose early the next morning and quickly got ready. Sometime in the middle of the night, she'd decided what she was going to do, and now she was anxious to follow through on it.

She'd downed two cups of coffee, but she was still bleary-eyed as she pulled into Connor's driveway, right behind Cam's car. It was only seven thirty in the morning, but she figured they'd be up because of Ava. And even if they weren't, too bad!

Inhaling deeply, she exited the car, and quietly closed the door, not wanting to give them advanced warning of her arrival. For a brief second, she questioned her decision to come there, but only for a second. She had to face this sometime, and now was as good as any.

She knocked on the door and waited. No answer. She knocked again, a little louder that time, and then she heard footsteps. *Here we go.*

The door opened with a whoosh, and the two women came face to face, staring at each other like they were in a western standoff until Cam reluctantly motioned her inside. In a way, the visual was even worse than Julia had imagined. Cam wasn't wearing sexy pajamas, but she was wearing one of Connor's T-shirts with the logo for O'Brien Brothers Landscaping printed on it and nothing else. The T-shirt hung to mid-thigh, but if Cam sat down, the shirt would probably show a glimpse of her underwear, assuming she was wearing any.

Even without makeup, Cam's skin glowed, which seemed unfair at seven thirty in the morning. Her hair was caught up in a swingy ponytail, and she was barefoot, her pink, polished toes looking entirely too comfortable in Connor's plush carpet. And to make matters worse, Cam was holding Ava on one hip, looking every bit the pretty young mom at home with her family on a sunny, Saturday morning.

The only saving grace was when Ava held out her chubby little arms in Julia's direction as if she wanted to be held by her. *HA!* But Cam ignored her daughter's request and eyed Julia haughtily like *she* was the intruder there.

Blood rang in her ears, but Julia managed to detect another sound—the shower running.

"Connor's in the shower," Cam said, confirming it.

"That's okay. I wanted to talk to you anyway."

"Well, as you can see, I'm kind of busy here. Ava was sick last night, and we were up late."

There was the dreaded *we* again. Julia was starting to hate that word.

"Yes, I know. How's she doing today?" Julia asked, temporarily setting aside her animosity and reminding herself that Ava was the innocent one here.

"Better, but she might be contagious, so you shouldn't get too close."

Ava looked fine from where Julia stood, but she got Cam's message loud and clear. Not wanting

Julia to get too close to her daughter is exactly what Cam wanted.

"I know what you're doing, Cam, and it's not going to work."

"What am I doing?"

"Trying to win Connor back."

The words floated in the air for a moment before Cam shrugged. "And what if I am?"

"You might think that because you had his baby, he'll take you back, but you're wrong. You screwed up when you screwed your boss, and Connor isn't going to forget that."

"Maybe not, but he might be able to forgive. If not for my sake, then for Ava's."

"What kind of mother uses her child as bait?"

"She's not bait. She's *our* child. That's right—ours. And Connor is going to want to do whatever's best for her."

"And you think what's best is if you three become a happy little family, right?"

Cam shrugged again.

"Connor already told me that's not going to happen."

Cam's eyes narrowed, and her smug smile instantly disappeared. "He may have said that to you to make you feel better, but that's not what he said last night."

Julia's heart began galloping in her chest. *Don't let her get to you. She's lying.*

"In fact, last night, when we were sitting in the living room drinking a beer, he said he'd consider letting Ava and me move in here for a while."

Julia studied Cam's face, looking for any indication that she was lying, but she didn't see one.

"Ask him yourself. He'll tell you," she said confidently.

Julia's head was spinning, and she thought she might faint. The shitty thing was she believed her. She could see where Connor might allow them to live there until Cam found a place of her own. And once Cam had him in her clutches, who knew what might happen. It wasn't out of the realm of possibility that he could fall in love with her again. People broke up and got back together all the time. Wasn't that the very reason Connor was skeptical of Alec?

She and Cam were still standing in the entranceway when she noticed the shower had shut off. She was debating about whether to wait for Connor to come out when, suddenly, he was standing there too, off to the side with a towel wrapped around his waist and damp hair.

When he saw Julia, his face lit up, but Julia noticed that Cam's did too as she openly perused his magnificent body from head to toe. Suddenly, it was all too much, and Julia had to escape. Turning around, she started to walk out when Connor called, "Julia, wait!"

Ignoring him, she pushed open the door and hurried to her car, moving quicker than she thought possible on her high-heeled wedges. She cursed herself for wearing them because she'd been trying to look pretty for him. What a joke!

"Julia, stop!" he shouted.

Ignoring him, she slid into the driver's seat, and then she noticed that he'd stepped onto his porch in the towel and was about to come after her. Behind him, Julia saw Cam and Ava standing in the doorway, watching the whole scene play out.

At that moment, all Julia's courage and determination disappeared, and all she wanted to do was get as far away from them as possible. Ignoring Connor's protests, she backed down the driveway faster than she probably should have and left him in a cloud of dust—literally. The last thing she saw was him waving his hands in front of his face to clear the dust away.

Heart pounding, her fingernails dug into the faux leather steering wheel. She was barely aware that she'd passed the turn-off to her street until she was already well past it. All she knew was that she didn't want Connor to find her, assuming he would come looking for her at all.

She thought about calling Harper, but it was her day off, and she was probably still in bed, maybe with Finn. Julia didn't want Finn to know what had happened, because, as Connor's brother and her friend, he'd be stuck in the middle. So, she went to the only other place she could think of—her parents' house.

Pulling into the driveway, she felt a wave of relief, and when her mom answered the door a minute later, she fell right into her open arms. It was then that the tears came, bursting out of her quicker than she could swipe them away.

Her mom led her over to the couch and sat down beside her, keeping one arm wrapped tightly around her shoulder while murmuring words of comfort. Once Julia's tears had subsided, Debra said, "What happened? Does this have anything to do with Connor?"

How do parents know things before you even tell them? Julia nodded, a fresh stream of tears trickling down her face.

"Do you want to tell me about it?" her mom asked softly.

Julia was glad that her dad worked on Saturdays and wasn't there to see her like this. If ever there was an "I told you so" moment, this was it, and she didn't want to hear it from both of them.

Sitting further back on the couch and wrapping her arms around her middle, she brought her mom up to date on all that had been happening with Connor. Debra listened intently, her expressions ranging from disbelief to empathy to outrage at Cam's behavior. When Julia had finished talking, her mom's first comment was, "That poor baby."

Huh? What about me? But it was exactly the sort of thing she would have expected from Debra, who hated to see anyone hurting, children most of all.

"I've seen so many kids from broken homes, and it never fails to make me sad," her mom explained. "Kids need both parents to succeed in this world."

Julia's eyes bugged out. "Are you saying that Connor and Cam should get back together?"

"No. That's not what I'm saying at all, especially since they don't love each other. That won't do Ava any good."

"Well, then what's the alternative?"

"Is that why you came over here? To ask for my advice?" Debra said.

"You sound surprised."

"That's because I can't remember the last time you took our advice. You've always followed your own path."

She was right, of course. Julia had prided herself on being her own person and not relying on anyone for direction. But she was out of her element here, and she had no idea which way to turn. "I just needed to talk to someone," she admitted.

"I'm glad you thought to come here. You haven't been around much lately, ever since you've…"

"Been dating Connor. Yeah, I know."

"I'm afraid we didn't get off to a very good start with him," Debra said, looking regretful. "Your dad especially."

It struck Julia that her mom hadn't referred to him as Dr. Lee that time. He was just "Dad," and maybe Julia had needed the reminder. Her parents weren't out to hurt her; they only wanted to protect her, just like most parents did with their children.

"Ava's so sweet. I'm really going to miss her."

Eyebrows raised, Debra said, "Are you breaking up with Connor?"

"Yes. No. God, I don't know!"

"I can understand that it would be difficult to take on another woman's child, but Ava's Connor's child too. Don't forget that."

"How can I? I've been reminded every day since Cam came back."

"What are you going to do?"

There it was, the million-dollar question. "I have no idea. I thought I knew this morning, but once I saw them together, looking like a cozy family—it was just too much. All I knew was that I had to get out of there."

"Maybe you should take a few days to think about it. Listen to your heart, and it won't lead you astray."

"Don't you have that saying embroidered on a towel or something?" Julia said.

Debra burst out laughing, and Julia chimed in.

"I believe it's on a cross-stitch I made," Debra said after their laughter had died down.

Picking up where they'd left off, Julia said, "The thing is, if I stay here, Connor will probably track me down, and I'm not ready to talk to him yet."

"So, go away for a few days. Go up to the lake house."

"The lake house! Why didn't I think of that?"

"I don't know, but you're welcome to use it anytime. You still have a key, don't you?"

Julia nodded, her enthusiasm growing by the second. "Yes, and I haven't been there in forever."

"Well, there you go. Take a few days to yourself, and you'll probably find the answers you're looking for."

"Sounds like another cross-stitch saying," Julia teased.

"Mom wisdom. You'll have it too someday."

And just like that, tears sprang to Julia's eyes again. Debra knew how much she wanted to be a mom and how devastated she'd been when Alec had said he didn't want kids. What irony that now that she had access to a baby, it wasn't hers. It was *theirs* as she'd been so glaringly reminded of earlier.

Even if she and Connor reconciled, could she love Cam's child? Could she look at Ava without thinking about how she'd come to be? And how would it work between her and Cam going forward? They obviously harbored a lot of resentment toward each other. Would that ever go away?

"You know what? A few days away is exactly what I need. I'm going to call Harper and see if she'll give me some time off."

"Great idea. I wish I'd thought of it," Debra said, patting Julia on the knee.

Standing up, Julia said, "Thanks for listening, Mom. And I'm sorry I haven't been around much lately. One way or another, I'm going to fix that."

"You just worry about you and Connor first, and then we'll go to work on your dad."

Bolstered by the knowledge that her mom was in her corner, Julia smiled, hugged her mom tight, and left.

On her way home, she called Harper, who answered on the first ring.

"There you are!" Harper exclaimed.

"Huh?"

"Connor's been looking all over for you. He just left here a few minutes ago after I swore I had no idea where you were."

"Good, and he won't find me if you agree to give me some time off."

"Wait a minute. Slow down. Time off for what? Where are you going?"

"To my parents' lake house, if you can spare me for a few days."

"Sure. That's no problem, but do you mind telling me what's going on? Connor didn't say much other than you're pissed at him and that you took off from his house earlier this morning."

It didn't surprise Julia that Connor hadn't said more. It was so typical for him to hide things, even from his family. But it made her even angrier.

As she drove, she told Harper what had happened, down to the details of what Cam had been wearing when she'd answered the door.

"That bitch!" Harper said.

Julia laughed, inwardly rejoicing that Harper was on her side despite her connection to the O'Briens.

"Was Finn there when Connor came over?"

"No, but he's pissed at Connor too."

"What for?"

"For not showing up to work this morning and not bothering to call."

"That's probably because he was too busy strutting around in a towel while Cam salivated all over him," Julia said.

"What are you going to do, Jules?"

"I don't know. That's why I'm going away for a few days, so I can wrap my head around this and decide whether or not Connor and I still have a chance."

Harper sighed. "Been there. I know exactly how you feel."

Harper had gone through something similar with Finn, although it'd had nothing to do with a baby. The ghost of her dead husband had come between her and Finn for a while until she'd decided that she didn't want to live without love—without Finn. Everything had worked out for the two of them, but Julia didn't hold out the same hope for her and Connor.

In Julia's situation, she had to think about four people—her, Connor, Ava, and Cam. And she'd already formed an attachment to Ava, which made the decision that much harder.

"Harper? Do me a favor."

"Anything."

"Don't tell Connor where I'm going. I can't see him right now. Promise me."

"What should I say if he asks, which I'm sure he will?"

"Tell him the truth. That I needed to get away for a few days and I'll talk to him when I get back." He should understand, given that he'd gone to Denver without her. She really didn't owe him any other explanation.

"Okay. I hope you find the answer you're looking for," Harper said.

"Me too." But right then, Julia had no idea what she wanted the answer to be.

Chapter 14

After searching everywhere for Julia and calling her cell phone repeatedly, Connor finally gave up. Wherever she was, she obviously didn't want to be found. She probably just needed a couple of hours to cool off, and then she'd call him. At least, that's what he hoped.

So, now he was on the job with his brothers, and they were laying mulch for their new customer, Mrs. Simmons, one of Harper's friends from her romance book club. At first, Connor had found it odd that Mrs. Simmons sat on her porch and watched them work, but he was too wrapped up in his troubles to care.

It had turned out to be a hot humid day, and his T-shirt was already soaked through. He'd been put in charge of shoveling mulch into wheelbarrows, and Finn and Liam were transporting it to the landscaped areas around the house. Mrs. Simmons had been supplying them with plenty of water and lemonade, and now she'd come outside with a tray of cookies.

"You boys are working so hard. I feel sorry for you in this heat," she said as she offered up freshly baked peanut butter cookies.

"It's our job. We're used to it," Connor said while choosing two cookies from the tray.

"But thank you very much for the drinks and cookies," Finn said as he came alongside them with the wheelbarrow.

After Mrs. Simmons had walked away, Finn turned to Connor and said, "Stop being such an asshole."

Connor scowled at him. "What are you talking about?"

"You know exactly what I'm talking about. First, you screwed up with Julia, and now you're taking it out on this sweet old lady. Lighten up!"

Connor didn't argue because Finn was right. Ever since his fallout with Julia, he'd been snapping at everyone in sight, including his brothers. After he'd chased Julia down the driveway in his towel, he'd gone back inside and snapped at Cam too. She'd played innocent, but he wondered what she'd said to Julia to make her take off in such a huff.

Cam had insisted that Julia hadn't liked seeing her in his T-shirt, but he knew it was more than that. When he'd asked Cam to spend the night, he hadn't completely thought it through. It was late, and Cam had been worried about waking up her parents, so he'd offered for her and Ava to stay over. He'd been trying to do the right thing by helping to take care of his sick child, but now he'd pissed off Julia—again! Maybe if he'd called her first, she wouldn't have been so mad, but then again, maybe not. It seemed like no matter what he did, he couldn't win right now.

"So, what did you do to Julia this morning?" Finn said as he came up for another load of mulch.

Mrs. Simmons was busy talking to Liam, but Connor lowered his voice anyway. "Cam and Ava spent the night at my place. Julia came over this morning, and Cam answered the door in my T-shirt. I think it pissed her off."

"You think?" Finn said, his eyes bugging out.

"I didn't know what else to do. It was late when we left the clinic, and Cam didn't want to disrupt her parents' sleep. She already feels guilty enough for staying there, so I offered up my place."

Finn wiped his forehead with the hem of his T-shirt while Connor scooped out the mulch. "Man, you've got to help Cam find her own place."

"I'm trying," Connor said, thrusting the shovel into the pile of mulch with a little more muscle than was completely necessary.

"Well, try harder. No woman wants to see her man's ex wearing his T-shirt."

"I get that, but I had no idea Julia would show up so early. I'd planned on going over to her place after I took a shower, but she beat me to it."

Just then, Liam wandered over with cookie crumbs on his lips. "Man, Mrs. Simmons makes some mean peanut butter cookies!"

Connor and Finn stopped what they were doing to stare at him.

"What? I was just building customer relations," Liam insisted.

"How many cookies did you eat?" Finn asked.

"Four or five. I wanted to make her feel good."

"Bullshit. You just like to eat!" Finn teased.

"What's going on over here, anyway? It's taking you girls a long time to load one wheelbarrow of mulch," Liam said.

"We're having a discussion," Finn replied.

"About chicks?"

Finn frowned. "How old are you, thirteen? They're called women, and yes, we were just talking about Julia."

"Ah. What did you do this time, bro?" Liam asked Connor.

"Shut up," Connor replied, flinging a shovelful of mulch into Liam's wheelbarrow.

"He had a sleepover with Cam, who was wearing his T-shirt when she answered the door to Julia," Finn said.

Liam tipped his head back and laughed. "Man, you really messed up!"

"It's not funny," Connor snarled. *Why do I work with my brothers again?*

"Are you and Cam…" Liam started to ask.

"No! But she's the mother of my child, and I can't just ignore her."

"That doesn't explain why she was wearing your shirt," Liam said, confused.

"Ava was sick last night, and Connor felt bad, so he let Cam and Ava spend the night at his house," Finn said. "If you'd have shown up at the restaurant last night like you said you would, you would have already known this."

Liam rolled his eyes. "I got busy."

"Busy doing what?" Finn asked.

"Or who?" Connor said.

"None of your business. I see enough of you guys during the day. I don't have to see you at night too," Liam said, and then he lifted up the wheelbarrow handles and walked away.

Raising his eyebrows, Finn said, "Hmm. It's interesting that McKayla didn't show up last night either. I wonder if…"

"No way. She hates him," Connor said, glad to change the subject.

"I'm not so sure of that," Finn said.

"You've been hanging around Harper too much. You're starting to sound like a girl."

"She's a woman, and I'd rather hang out with her than you two buttheads."

"Now you sound like Liam," Connor said just as Liam sauntered back over.

"Huh?" Liam said upon hearing his name.

"Nothing," Finn said, walking away with his wheelbarrow.

Finally, Connor thought, rolling his shoulders to release the tension. Finn always gave him a hard time, but this time, he deserved it. He should have handled things differently with Julia, and then he wouldn't be in this mess.

"So, what are you going to do about Cam and Julia?" Liam asked, wiping the sweat from his brow with the back of his hand.

"Not you too," Connor huffed.

"Hey, I'm just asking."

"I don't know what to do. That's the problem. I have a kid now, and I need to be there for her, but if I alienate Cam, she could take Ava away from me. I can't let that happen."

"So, where does that leave Julia?"

"I want her in my life too, but I'm not sure how to juggle it all. And right now, Julia doesn't want anything to do with me."

Liam shrugged. "You don't know that for sure. Sometimes, chicks act like they don't want you, but they really do."

"Are you speaking from experience, or is that wishful thinking?" Finn asked when he'd come up behind them.

"Whatever," Liam said, and turning his ballcap backward, he hurried off with his load.

"Something's up with him," Finn said.

"Yeah, maybe," Connor replied, still too distracted by his own problems to worry about Liam.

"So, do you want my advice or not?" Finn asked as Connor scooped him another load.

"I have a feeling you're going to give it to me whether I want it or not."

"You're right. So, here goes. No relationship is perfect, and you're gonna have problems. But if you care about Julia, I mean *really* care about her, you'll fix this."

"You gonna sew that on a T-shirt?" Connor said sarcastically.

"If I did, I wouldn't let my *ex*-girlfriend wear it."

"Enough about the stupid T-shirt! She didn't have any pajamas, and it was the only thing I had to offer her."

"Well, maybe next time, offer her a pair of sweatpants to go with it," Finn said and then walked away. And guy talk was officially over.

Later that night, Connor sat in his empty house and nursed a beer. He'd tried calling Julia again after work, but the call had gone right to voicemail. She must have updated her message during the day, because now it said that she'd be out of town for a few days and she'd return the call when she got back.

Great! Now he'd have to wait three days to talk to her, and he sucked at waiting. It was driving him crazy that he couldn't talk to her. He wasn't even sure what he'd say when he saw her, but he just knew he had to see her. He couldn't let her think that anything had gone on between him and Cam last night, because nothing had. Although, if he'd been open to it, something might have happened.

Cam hadn't overtly come on to him; however, a few of the looks she'd given him as they'd sat together drinking beer…well, let's just say he'd seen those looks before. She'd sat cross-legged on the couch, his shirt barely covering her lower half, and eyed him up like a hot fudge sundae that she was dying to take a bite of.

But all he'd been able to think about was how he'd wished Julia was there instead. Looking at Cam from across the room (he hadn't dared sit next to her lest she get the wrong idea), he hadn't been the least bit attracted to her. Sure, she was pretty in a Barbie doll sort of way, but she didn't do it for him anymore.

He much preferred Julia's silky black hair, her deep brown eyes that reminded him of the Hershey bars she loved so much, and her curvy body that she spent entirely too much time trying to hide. He'd rather have heard her hearty, unselfconscious laugh and seen that smile that lit up the room than listen to

Cam rattle on about nothing while she tossed her blonde hair around and gave him come-hither looks.

If she'd thought she could seduce him, she'd been dead wrong, and by the end of the night, he'd suspected she knew that. After making sure Ava was sound asleep, he'd retreated to his bedroom, where he'd locked the door behind him. He hadn't done it to keep himself in but to keep Cam out just in case she got any ideas about slipping into his bed at night. At first, he hadn't believed Julia when she'd said that Cam was trying to win him back, but now he understood. Whenever he'd brought up Julia's name, Cam had stopped talking or averted her eyes like she didn't want to acknowledge that Julia was important to him.

But she was, more than he wanted to admit. He understood that she was hurt and angry, and he hated that he'd been the one to cause it. When he'd first met her, he'd played his usual game of flirting with her until she'd agreed to go out with him. But he wasn't playing a game anymore. He cared about her— a lot. And the last thing he wanted was to hurt her, but how could he convince her if she wouldn't even talk to him?

His brothers were right—he'd really screwed up this time. And he spent the rest of the night wondering how he was going to fix it.

Chapter 15

Julia hadn't realized how uptight she was until she unlocked the door of her parents' lake house and stepped inside. It was only then, after an uneventful four-hour drive, that she took a deep breath and began to relax.

And how could she not? The "cottage" was more charming than she'd remembered, and the views of Walloon Lake were spectacular. She tried to remember the last time she'd been there and realized it had been a few years ago when she was still with Alec.

He'd stayed in the room next to hers, and she recalled trying to convince him to sneak into her room at night, but he'd refused. He'd never been much of a risk taker, and he hadn't wanted to ruin his "good standing with her parents." She'd wondered if his future career as a doctor was more important to him than her, and looking back, she believed it had been. He'd probably loved her in his own way, but his relationship with her father had probably been just as important, maybe even more so.

What a difference between him and Connor. There was no doubt in her mind that Connor would have snuck into her room. Their relationship was based on passion and emotions, and he wouldn't have let her parents stop him from coming to her. Too bad the same passion that had brought them together was now tearing them apart.

Shaking her head to clear her runaway thoughts, she rolled her suitcase into the upstairs bedroom she usually used and began unpacking. Her room faced the lake, and looking out the window, she took in the shimmering blue water and cloudless sky. She'd lucked out; the weather forecast called for warm temperatures and no rain for the next several days, and she planned to take full advantage of it.

After she'd unpacked, she changed from her jeans and t-shirt into a tank top and shorts. Grabbing her book from her tote bag, and her phone, she went back downstairs and into the kitchen. Her parents must have been there recently because there were a few beverages in the refrigerator and some non-perishable snacks in the pantry.

She selected a Snapple and a package of graham crackers, unlocked the sliding glass door to the deck, and stepped outside. It was the third weekend in May, and there were several boats on the lake even though the water was still too cold for swimming. She thought about taking her parents' pontoon boat out later, but for now, she was content to lie back in a lounge chair and bask in the sun.

For the next two hours, that's exactly what she did. She drank lemonade, munched on crackers, and let her mind go. She even managed to read a few chapters in her latest mystery novel, which was more than she'd read in quite a while.

"See? This is perfect," she said as she stretched out her legs and wiggled her toes. Other than the sounds from passing boats and birds chirping in the nearby trees, there was nothing but peace and quiet. This was exactly what she'd needed.

Just then, her phone vibrated on the small glass-topped table beside her chair. She'd switched the phone to vibrate mode even though she had no intention of answering it. Her curiosity had prevented her from turning it off completely because she still wanted to know who was calling—specifically Connor.

He'd left a few messages earlier in the day, but her phone had been quiet for hours. She figured he'd be working with his brothers, but now it was approaching six o'clock, and he should be home. Unless he'd gone apartment hunting with Cam again. *Cam.* Even the name made her stomach clench.

She waited until her phone stopped buzzing before she picked it up and listened to the message.

Hey. I know you're mad at me, but I really wish you'd pick up. I hate talking on these things.

There was a long pause, and then he continued.

I know it didn't look good, what you saw this morning, but I told you Cam was staying over. She didn't have any clothes with her...I mean, other than the ones she had on, so I loaned her a T-shirt to sleep in.

Another long pause.

Damn! I was hoping you'd answer so I didn't have to explain this to a machine. Anyway, I didn't expect you to come over so early. I was in the shower getting ready so I could come over to your house.

Silence.

I swear to you that nothing happened. Cam slept in the spare room with Ava, and I slept in my room. That was it.

A heavy sigh.

There's more I'd like to say, but I'm not going to say it to a machine. I've already talked longer on this thing than I thought I would. I might not have the right to ask you for a favor, but I'm going to anyway. Please hear me out, Jules. Call me back. Please.

And then he hung up.

Julia listened to the message again just in case she'd missed anything. Afterward, she thought about what he'd said and realized he hadn't told her anything she didn't already know. Her worry wasn't that he and Cam had slept together (she refused to believe that), but whether what Cam had said was true. Was she moving in with him?

She understood that he hadn't wanted to talk to a machine, but still, there was nothing in his message that soothed her. Nothing about missing her or wondering where she'd gone or when she was coming back. Nothing other than him defending his actions, as usual. And that wasn't enough. Not anymore. She'd accepted his apologies before, but this time was different. This time, she needed stronger evidence that he really wanted to make this work.

Maybe that was wrong of her. Maybe she was expecting too much too soon, but she didn't think so. Before she poured any more energy into their relationship, she needed to know how he really felt about her, about Cam, and about the future. Until then, she wasn't going to give any more of herself than she already had.

Later that evening, Julia went into the charming town of Petoskey to get some dinner. Deciding that she didn't want to sit inside on such a beautiful night, she bought a roast beef sandwich at a popular deli and took it down to the park that lined the shores of Little Traverse Bay. There, she found a quiet spot and sat down at a picnic table overlooking the water.

She was busy eating her sandwich and watching the seagulls circle overhead and hadn't noticed that anybody was nearby until she felt something brush up against her leg. Startled, she turned to find the source and had to look down. At her feet, there was a large plastic ball and a little girl, maybe two years old, staring up at her.

"Ball," the little girl said and pointed. Just then, a man, who Julia presumed was the girl's father, rushed up beside her.

"Sorry about that," he said and scooped up the girl and the ball.

"No worries," Julia said, smiling up at him. She couldn't help but notice how good looking he was as he stood there backlit by the sun, his light-brown hair ruffling in the breeze and a sweet smile on his face.

"Chips," the little girl said, pointing at Julia's Doritos bag.

"Would you like one?" Julia said, holding the bag out.

"Oh, no. That's okay. We don't want to interrupt your dinner," the man said.

"It's fine. I don't need all these anyway," Julia said.

He set the girl back down, and she scrambled up on the seat next to Julia and plunged her little hand into the Doritos bag.

Julia laughed to see that the girl was as big a fan of chips as she was.

Looking uncomfortable, the man took a seat on the other side of the girl since she wasn't about to settle for just one chip.

"What's your name?" Julia asked.

"Scott," the man said, followed by, "Oh. You meant my daughter. This is Ava."

What are the chances? Julia gripped the edge of the table to steady herself. "Ava. What a pretty name."

"Thank you," Ava said before stuffing another chip in her mouth.

Scott looked at Julia curiously, obviously having noticed her reaction.

"I know an Ava too," Julia explained, "but she's only five months old."

"Your daughter?" Scott asked.

"No. My boyfriend's daughter." *If I can still call him that.*

"Ah."

Just then, Ava scooted off the bench and started playing with her ball again.

"Stay near me this time," Scott instructed before turning his attention back to Julia. "Thanks for the chips. I hope we didn't disturb you too much."

"Not at all," she said and smiled.

"Say goodbye to the nice lady," Scott said to Ava.

"Bye, nice lady," Ava called, an orange outline from the Doritos lining her little pink lips.

Too choked up to speak, Julia waved, and then she watched them walk away, Scott clasping his daughter's hand tightly while she kicked the ball in front of her.

They were nearing the parking lot when a woman approached them with her arms outstretched, and Ava ran into them.

The mother, Julia assumed, noticing the look of pure joy on the woman's face as she hugged Ava to her chest. After she set Ava down, she reached up on her tiptoes and gave Scott a quick kiss on the lips. Julia was still watching the happy reunion when, suddenly, Ava pointed in Julia's direction and started waving.

She hated to be caught staring, but it was too late, and then all three of them waved to her before they turned away and got into the car that the woman had driven up in.

After they left, Julia sat there for a few more minutes, her mind whirring. Was it possible for her to be that happy with Connor and his daughter? Did it really matter that Ava wasn't hers? Having Ava didn't mean they couldn't have their own children someday. But would Connor want that?

Ugh! She was no closer to having her answers than she'd been before coming there. If only she would have kept her chips to herself! But she couldn't help it. She was like a kid magnet. She loved them, and they gravitated toward her too—kids, not chips. It had been like that ever since she could remember. And she'd felt that way with Ava too—Connor's Ava.

No matter what happened between her and Connor, she would never blame that little girl. She wondered what Ava would be like as a two-year-old, a five-year-old, a teenager. Would she be free-spirited and spontaneous like her father? What would her interests be? She was already so pretty that Julia could just imagine what she might look like when she was older. Connor was in for some trouble, that was for sure.

Suddenly, Julia realized that she was sitting there all alone, smiling. The thought of Connor and Ava was making her smile even after how upset she'd been. Go figure! Shaking her head, she cleaned up the remnants of her dinner and left the park. When she got back to the lake house, it was dark, and she struggled to fit the key into the lock. She hadn't expected to be out so late, and she'd forgotten to leave the porch light on. Swearing, she finally got the door open and stepped inside. Locking the door behind her, she slipped off her shoes, hung her purse on the coat rack, and then walked into the living room to turn on a light.

But she didn't have to because, suddenly, a lamp flicked on, and Julia's hands flew to her chest in terror.

"Sorry. I didn't mean to scare you," he said, rising up from the chair.

Chapter 16

"Ohmigod, Alec! What are you doing here?" Julia said, her heart still pumping overtime. She flicked on another light just to make sure it was really him.

"Your dad was worried, and he asked me to come up and check on you."

Julia slumped down on the couch, taking a moment to catch her breath while Alec sat back down in the chair across from her.

"My dad asked you to drive all the way up here to check on me?" she asked, incredulous.

Alec nodded. "I was with Dr. Lee at his office this morning when your mom called to let him know that you drove up here. He thought it was odd that you came here alone, and he sort of asked me to come and see if you were okay."

"Sort of?"

"Well, I could tell how concerned he was, and I guess I kind of volunteered."

Julia sighed. "Why would you do that?"

He shrugged. "Even though we're not together, I still care about you. Besides, it's not like it's a hardship. This place is awesome."

She wasn't sure whom she was madder at—her dad or Alec. It was hard to be too upset with Alec, who had just driven four hours to check on her; however, she wasn't happy about it either.

"I purposely came here to be alone for a few days," she said, determined to keep her anger in check.

"Why? Is something wrong?"

Tapping her fingers on her leg, she debated how to answer. While it really wasn't any of his business, maybe it would be a good opportunity to reiterate that she had no interest in getting back together with Alec. If he thought driving up here would change that, he was sorely mistaken.

"Connor and I are having some…issues," she said.

Alec didn't look surprised, and she wondered how much he already knew. Since Alec had been in her dad's office when her mom had called, he could have easily overheard the whole sordid story.

"I can't say I'm completely surprised," Alec said, confirming her suspicions.

"What is that supposed to mean?" Even though she was uncertain about where she and Connor stood, she still felt the need to defend her choice to be with him. She didn't appreciate first her dad and now Alec passing unfair judgment on a man they hardly knew.

Rubbing his hands on his pant legs as if to gather courage, Alec said, "He just looks like trouble, Jules. He doesn't look like the kind of guy you would be interested in."

Angrily, she pushed herself up from the couch, planted her hands on her hips, and said, "Compared to who—you?"

Alec shook his head. "I didn't say that."

153

"But that's what you meant. I'm so sick of everyone telling me that Connor's not good enough for me."

Alec stood up and started walking toward her with his arms outstretched as if to say, "I come in peace."

She'd just taken a step back when suddenly there was a pounding on the front door that stopped them both in their tracks.

"Open up, Jules. It's me."

Holy shit! Eyes wide, Julia glanced from the front door to Alec and then back to the door again. *What are the chances?*

"I'm not leaving until you open the door," he said loudly. "I'll camp out here all night if I have to."

"Aren't you going to let him in?" Alec asked, breaking her out of panic mode.

"Why should I?" She must have spoken louder than she realized, because she was given an answer from her angry visitor.

"Because I drove four hours to talk to you, and I'm not going anywhere until we do!"

Julia stared at Alec for a moment, wondering if she should ask him to hide for his own safety.

"You might as well open the door," Alec said resignedly.

"You're of no help at all, you know that?" she huffed before turning away and walking toward the door.

"Stop yelling. I'm coming!" she shouted. Good thing the houses were spread far enough apart that the neighbors couldn't hear all the ruckus. At least she hoped not.

Squaring her shoulders and inhaling deeply, Julia flung open the door to reveal her visitor.

She and Connor stared at each other for a few beats, acting like they hadn't seen each other in days rather than a matter of hours.

His hair looked rumpled, like he'd been shoving his hands through it during the drive up. There was no softness in his steely blue eyes, nor in the grim set of his mouth. The only casual thing about him were his clothes—a black T-shirt that showed the bottom edge of his tattoo, worn-in blue jeans with rips in the knees, and a pair of black Converse that had been hastily tied. He looked like a man on a mission— a mission to get to her—and the realization took her breath away.

"Hi," Connor said after he'd given her a thorough perusal too. Then, as if he realized there was another presence in the room, he looked over her shoulder and saw Alec standing there.

Alec cleared his throat noisily and said, "Hello."

"I wasn't talking to you," Connor hissed, and then zeroing in on Julia, he said, "What the hell is *he* doing here?"

"I could ask you the same thing," she said, although she moved aside to let him in.

Connor stepped into the light and surveyed the scene, looking for what, she wasn't sure. Evidence that she was cheating on him with Alec? What a bizarre turn of events. Just hours ago, she'd been the one worried about him and Cam, and now the tables were turned. She wasn't above keeping him in misery for just a few minutes longer.

In a show of male dominance, Connor stepped further into the room and glared at Alec. It would have been comical if Julia hadn't been so pissed at them. Alec looked a bit frightened, and he took a big step backward.

"Dr. Lee asked me to come and check on her," Alec hurriedly explained, as if that would give him a free pass.

"Oh, right. And I bet you didn't mind one bit," Connor snarled.

Alec opened his mouth to reply, but Julia interrupted.

"Stop it, Connor. Stop trying to intimidate him with your peacocking!"

Both men stopped and stared at her.

"Peacocking?" Connor said, his lips curling up in a slight smile.

"Or whatever you want to call it," she hissed.

"Look. It's obvious that you two have a lot to talk about, so I'll just leave you to it," Alec said and started to walk toward the door.

"NO!" Julia shouted, surprising all three of them.

Lowering her voice, she said, "It's late, and it's a long drive. I would feel terrible if you fell asleep at the wheel and got into an accident. You can leave in the morning."

Connor gaped at her and looked like he was about to protest, but she didn't give him the chance.

"And you can stay too, but I'm not talking to you tonight. It's late, and I'm tired. I would have already been in bed if I didn't have so many uninvited guests."

Connor visibly backed down even though he didn't look happy about it in the least.

"There are two perfectly comfortable couches in here, and you two can arm wrestle over them if you want to, but I'm going to bed!" With that, she turned on her bare feet and stomped out of the room, leaving the men standing there, flummoxed.

When she reached her bedroom, she slammed the door with a flourish and locked it before flopping back onto the bed. It took awhile for her heart rate to slow and the blood to stop ringing in her ears, and then she was hit with an unexpected bout of laughter. Burying her face in a pillow, she laughed hysterically for a few minutes until she got herself back under control.

If only she had a spy cam to see what Connor and Alec were up to. Just the thought of it had her laughing again, but then she heard voices coming up through the vent beside her bed. The men were talking without bothering to keep their voices down, unaware that she could hear them.

Quietly crawling off the bed, Julia sprawled out on the floor and put her ear to the vent. Yep— it still worked, just like when she was a kid. She and her best friend, Karen, used to do this when they wanted to hear what Karen's older brother and his girlfriend were saying. What they'd usually heard had been a lot more kissing than talking, but this was better. This was her ex-boyfriend, the man she'd almost married, and her current boyfriend talking about her. This was juicier than spying on Karen's older brother by far.

"I'm on to you, Alec," Connor said. "You might be fooling Julia, but you can't fool me."

"I don't know what you're talking about," Alec replied.

"Don't play dumb. You're going to be a doctor, for Christ's sake."

"It's just like I said. Her parents were worried, and they asked me to check on her. That's all there is to it."

"So, you don't have feelings for her anymore? You really expect me to believe that?"

"What about you?" Alec countered, his voice sounding more venomous than she'd ever heard.

"What about me?"

"I heard that you're living with your ex-girlfriend and that she had your baby."

Julia's fingers clenched the carpet. So, Alec did know the whole story. But what was surprising was how he wasn't backing down. She would have never expected that from him.

"I'm not *living* with her. Cam spent one night because our baby was sick and she needed my help."

"Let me get this straight. Julia's supposed to believe that you don't have feelings for Cam, the mother of your child, yet you can stand there and accuse me of still having feelings for Julia?"

Julia's heart pounded while she waited for Connor's reply. Not that she needed Alec to fight her battles, but she had to give him some credit for standing up for her like that.

"My situation is different. Cam cheated on me, and I left her and never looked back. Yes, she had my baby, but I have no interest in reconciling with her— *ever.*"

Julia breathed out, and it was so loud she wondered for a moment if they'd heard it. But after a few seconds, they continued talking like nothing was amiss.

"And what about Julia? What are your intentions with her now that you have a child?"

"That's really none of your business."

"I'm just asking because I don't want to see her get hurt—again."

Again? Is he referring to himself? A moment later, she got her answer.

"I loved her, but I hurt her pretty bad," Alec said. "I'll always regret that."

"Well, I don't plan on hurting her," Connor said, his voice softer now.

"We don't always plan on hurting the people we love, but it can still happen," Alec said.

Love? Connor never said anything about love.

"Julia means a lot to me. She's important to me. I'm not going to lose her."

Connor hadn't used the word love, but there was no mistaking the emotion in his voice, and it made her throat constrict. It was the closest he'd come to sharing his feelings about her. Too bad he was sharing them with her ex-boyfriend instead.

"You seem pretty sure of yourself."

"That's because I am."

"Sounds like you're a little too cocky."

I used to accuse him of that too.

"Not cocky. Confident," Connor stated.

After a moment of silence, Julia wondered if they were done talking, but then Alec piped up again.

"I didn't come here to get between you two," he said, his voice clear and calm. "I came because I was worried about her. Julia's one of the greatest people I've ever known, and she deserves the best."

"I agree."

"I'm not sure that you're what's best for her," Alec said.

"That's for her to decide."

Julia lay there for a few more minutes, waiting to hear more, but other than some rustling sounds from them getting settled, there wasn't anything else. She carefully rose from the floor and slipped back into bed, still wearing her clothes from earlier.

She lay there in silence for a while, listening to the sound of the wind in the trees outside her window and replaying what she'd overheard. She hoped that Connor was being truthful about Cam not living with him and hadn't been trying to cover it up in front of Alec. Alec might be the one who was studying to become a doctor, but Connor was no dummy. He'd have known that anything he said to Alec would have a good chance of getting back to her parents. So, until she heard it from him directly, she wasn't going to get too excited.

The same went for his confession about not wanting to lose her. She'd heard the conviction in his voice, but it would mean more once he said it to her face. And he probably would have if she hadn't banned them both to the living room. But what else was she supposed to do? It was already awkward enough having them both there. She couldn't very well haul Connor up to her room to talk, even though that's exactly what she'd wanted to do when he'd shown up at the door. Well, that and a few other things, if she were being honest.

What was it about him? How had he gotten under her skin so quickly to where it was difficult to imagine her life without him? And why was it that she could easily envision her, him, and Ava having fun together in the park, just like the family of three she'd seen earlier? Interestingly enough, she didn't see Cam anywhere in that picture, and that was the problem. Because, no matter how much Julia wanted to be with Connor and Ava, she'd have to accept Cam's presence in her life too.

Glancing at the clock, Julia saw that it was after midnight. Instead of getting out of bed to find her pajamas, she decided to peel off her clothes and sleep in her bra and underwear. She didn't want the floor to creak and alert the men that she was still up. Wriggling out of her clothes, she laid them at the end of the bed and then crawled underneath the covers.

The best thing she could do was try and get some sleep since her troubles would still be there in the morning—both of them!

Chapter 17

Connor was tired of waiting. He'd spent an entire day and night trying to get to Julia, and now that he'd tracked her down, he was anxious to talk to her. Alec had had the decency to leave early that morning, rousing Connor from his sleep to say, "Be good to her," before placing the blanket he'd used neatly at the foot of the couch and departing.

Somehow, Connor had managed to sleep through the night even though Alec's snoring had threatened to keep him awake. And now with Alec gone, he could finally talk to Julia, assuming she was awake.

She hadn't come downstairs yet, and he wondered if she was delaying their confrontation. Pushing himself to an upright position, he ran his fingers through his hair and realized he'd peeled off his shirt and socks sometime during the night.

Oh well. This is how she gets me.

Not bothering to walk softly, he took the stairs two at a time until he reached the top. He glanced both ways down the hall, not sure which room was hers, and stopped to listen for any sounds. Nothing.

Trying the handle of the door closest to him, he pushed it open and peered inside. The room was a home office equipped with a large cherrywood desk, leather office chair, and floor-to-ceiling bookcases.

Connor closed the door and moved on to the next room, which was a feminine-looking bedroom decorated with white wicker furniture, floral accents, and a white bookcase. This must have been Julia's room when she was a child. Curious, he walked up to the bookcase and ran his eyes over the titles: Nancy Drew mysteries, the Hardy Boys, and an assortment of other childhood classics.

"Snooping?" Julia said from behind him.

Connor had his hand on a copy of *Are You There God? It's Me, Margaret* when he spun around, and the book fell to the floor.

Glancing down at the title, Julia laughed. "Thinking of doing some reading?"

"No," Connor said, quickly inserting the book back into position on the shelf. "Are these in alphabetical order?"

"Yes. Why?"

"Just wondered," he said, scratching the back of his head.

"I'm an organized person."

"Yeah. I noticed."

"So, if you weren't coming up here to read, what were you doing?"

"Looking for you."

"Well, here I am."

Connor took a moment to look at her—really look at her. She'd obviously just woken up, since she didn't have a stitch of makeup on. Her hair was done up in a messy bun, she wore a pair of gray shorts and a University of Michigan T-shirt, and her feet were bare.

She looked adorable and sexy at the same time, and he was suddenly extremely glad that Alec had already left.

"Where's Alec?" she said as if she'd read his mind.

"He left about an hour ago."

"Hmm. Did he leave on his own, or did you kick him out?"

"He woke me up to say he was leaving." He left out the part about Alec's warning.

"Hmm," Julia repeated as if she didn't quite believe him.

"I swear," Connor said solemnly, placing a hand over his heart for good measure. But the move seemed to have a different effect as her eyes focused in on his bare chest and then drifted up to his tattoo. She quickly looked away, but not before he saw the flicker of desire in her eyes. *Good. That's one point in my favor.*

"So. You came here to talk, but before we do, I need some coffee," Julia said, turning away and walking out of the room.

He had no choice but to follow her, although he didn't mind the view. His hands itched to reach out and touch her. Under different circumstances, he would have scooped her up in his arms and carried her back to bed. But then Alec's words rang in his head. *Be good to her.* He was pretty sure Alec hadn't meant to strip her naked and take her up against the wall, so Connor kept his hands to himself as he followed her down the stairs.

Once they were in the kitchen, he sat down at the table while she bustled around making coffee. Then, body bent into the refrigerator, she asked, "Do you want anything?"

Hell yeah, I do. Licking his lips, he said, "Water is fine."

Why was it that seeing Julia like this, fresh out of bed, was more stimulating to him than seeing Cam all glammed up, or any other woman for that matter? There was just something about Julia that he found irresistible.

"Here ya go," she said, setting a bottle of water before him.

Catching a whiff of her sleepy scent, he suppressed the urge to pull her onto his lap. He felt like a horny teenager as he watched her move around the kitchen, hoping for a glimpse down her shirt.

When she finally sat down across from him, he felt relieved. At least they were in the same room together without any possibility of being interrupted. Connor had told Cam that he'd be out of touch for a couple of days and that she could call one of his brothers if she needed anything. She'd pouted and asked where he was going, but he'd kept silent. He needed to see Julia without any interference from Cam this time. And here was the perfect place.

The sliding glass door off the kitchen offered an expansive view of Walloon Lake, and there were already a few boats bobbing on the water. Probably fishermen hoping for an early catch. Connor wouldn't have minded being out there himself, but right now, he had more important things to do.

"This is a great place," he said, deciding to start with an icebreaker.

"It is. I've been coming here since I was a kid, but I haven't been much lately."

"How come?"

"Too busy, I guess."

"I take it Alec's been here before too," he said, unable to keep the jealousy out of his voice.

"Yes, when we were dating. I never expected him to show up last night, though."

"I believe you," he said, and he did. He could tell that she was no longer interested in her ex, and now he had to convince her that he felt the same.

Julia nodded and took another sip of coffee, her hands wrapped tightly around the mug like she was holding onto a life raft. He hated that he'd caused her to be wary of him, and he was desperate to put an end to it.

"The other day, with Cam…"

"She said she was moving in with you," Julia blurted out, her eyes boring into his.

"That's not true."

"She sounded pretty adamant about it. Are you sure you didn't give her that impression?"

Scraping his hand across his stubbled cheek, he said, "I might have, but I didn't mean to."

"You either said it or you didn't, Connor. Which is it?"

"I said that she could stay for a few days if she needed to, but that I wanted her to find an apartment as soon as possible."

"That's not what she said."

"Are you surprised?"

"No, but it proves what I've thought all along. She still wants you, Connor, and it's not just to help out with Ava."

Leaning forward, he placed one hand atop hers and said, "But I don't want her. Does that count for anything?"

She studied him carefully before responding, "Have you told her that?"

She'd stumped him there. "I assumed she already knew. She knows you and I are dating, and I haven't done anything to encourage her."

"Except invite her to stay over and loan her your T-shirt," she said sarcastically.

Her eyes had narrowed to slits, but he still thought she looked sexy. "That was a mistake, but I was just thinking of Ava. She seemed so small and helpless when we were at the clinic, and even though nothing was seriously wrong, I didn't feel right being apart from her."

Julia sighed. "I get that part. I really do. How is she feeling, by the way?"

"Much better. It was just an ear infection, but the antibiotic seems to be helping."

"Good."

"Julia?"

"Yeah?"

He rubbed his thumb back and forth over the soft skin on the back of her hand and gazed at her imploringly. "I'm sorry. I really am. I'm sorry that having Cam stay over hurt you, and I'm sorry for whatever she said to you. But you have to believe me when I tell you that I don't have any desire to get back together with her. None. It's you that I want and only you. I want this to work between us, and I'm willing to do whatever it takes to make that happen. Please believe me."

Julia swallowed hard, and her eyes misted over. "This whole situation is really hard, Connor. Harder than I thought it would be."

"I understand."

"How can you when I'm having a difficult time understanding it myself? Ava's adorable, and I'd love to spend more time with her, but…"

"No buts, Julia. We can make it work. I promise."

"But what about Cam? Is she going to accept me wanting to spend time with her daughter? What if she tries to take Ava away from you again?"

He smiled because there she was, thinking about everyone else but herself. "I won't let that happen. I'll talk to Cam and make her understand that it's you I want. You and Ava."

"You make it sound so easy."

"Listen. Cam has her pride. She might have thought that she could lure me back in, but once she realizes that I'm not interested, she'll back off. And I doubt she'll take Ava away again, because she needs my help."

"What about her sister in Colorado?"

"I don't think she really wants to move there, Jules. Her life is here. Her job is here. I think she just went there for a while out of desperation."

Seeing that he had a lot more convincing to do, he pushed back his chair and went around to her side of the table. Kneeling down next to her, he slanted her chair so she was facing him and placed his palms on her thighs.

"What do I have to do to make you believe that it's you I want? Tell me. I'll do anything."

"Anything?" she said, perking up.

"Name it."

"Well, for starters you could take me out to breakfast."

He tipped his head back and laughed, feeling better than he had in hours. If his girl wanted to eat, then he'd be happy to feed her. And maybe afterward, she'd want something else from him. Something that would allow him to show her how much he wanted, needed, and l—

Whoa. Hold on. Do I love her? Did I just think that?

"Connor? Everything okay?"

Nodding, he replied, "Yes. Everything's fine." Never mind that his hands were sweating and his heart was racing. She didn't need to know that. Wiping his palms on his shorts, he said, "C'mon. Let's go eat."

Chapter 18

Soon they were driving to Petoskey in Connor's Jeep. It was another beautiful day, and he'd taken the top down, so the breeze ruffled their hair. Julia's mood had improved drastically. She was in a place that she loved with a man that she l—liked a lot (*Was I just thinking love?*), and she was going out to breakfast. All those factors combined made it impossible to stay mad. But there was something else she was dying to know.

"Who told you where I was?" she asked.

"Harper."

"I knew it! She's terrible at keeping secrets."

"Believe me, it was hard to get it out of her. I had to make all kinds of promises before she'd tell me."

"Wait a minute. She knew that I was going to my parents' lake house, but I never gave her the address."

Connor was wearing his aviators, and she couldn't see his eyes when he replied, "I know. I had to go to your mom for that."

"What?! She caved too?"

"Yep."

"But I told her that I wanted to be alone. I can't believe she sent you up here."

"She tried to talk me out of it, but I can be pretty persuasive when I want to be. That and I think she took pity on me."

Julia laughed. "Now, that, I can believe."

"I like your mom."

"You might like my dad too if you give him a chance."

"I think he's still hung up on you being with Alec."

"That isn't going to happen."

"Have you told your dad that?"

She'd said the very same thing to Connor about Cam. "I guess I need to sit down and have a talk with him."

Connor shrugged. "Family stuff is tricky. Do whatever you need to do, but in the end, as long as we're together, I'll be happy."

He'd said it so matter-of-factly, yet his words took her breath away. A few minutes later, he pulled into the parking lot of Big Boy Restaurant on Spring Street. As she was getting out of the Jeep, he came around and took her hand before leading her inside.

"How'd you know I like Big Boy?" she asked, enjoying the feel of their hands clasped together.

"Because I know you. You're probably going to order pancakes, a side of bacon, and a Diet Coke. Am I right?"

Before she could answer, they were approached by a hostess. "Table for two, please," Connor said.

After they were seated, Julia said, "Am I that predictable?"

"Not in all things, but with food, yes."

When the waitress returned, Connor ordered for them, and then he smiled at Julia across the table. "Don't be mad at Harper or your mom, okay? If you're going to be mad at anyone, be mad at me for badgering them until they gave in."

But with each passing second, her anger was dissipating. He'd come all the way there just to talk to her when he could have waited two more days. And he'd gone to her parents' house, which couldn't have been easy. Not when he knew that they weren't his biggest fans, although her mom seemed to be coming around.

"I'm not mad at them. I was just surprised, that's all. I expected to have a few days all to myself."

"Do you want me to leave?" he asked, his expression betraying his words.

She shook her head. "No."

"Good to hear."

Satisfied with her decision, they dug into their breakfast, and needing the reprieve, they talked about lighter topics.

"So, Liam's making a fool of himself over McKayla," Connor said between bites of scrambled egg.

"Oh yeah? What's he doing?"

"He keeps asking her out, and she keeps turning him down, but he's not taking the hint."

"Sounds familiar."

Connor laughed. "Yeah. I guess we O'Brien brothers are a stubborn bunch."

"Not to mention hot!" Oops, she hadn't meant to say that, even though it was true.

"But I'm the hottest one, right?" he teased.

"Of course, and you're not at all cocky. Just…"

"Confident," they said in unison.

This felt good. Laughing, smiling, and teasing each other instead of being at each other's throats. Even if it was a temporary reprieve from reality, it was much needed, and Julia decided to soak it up while they could. Who knew what was waiting for them back at home?

"Now that you're here, what should we do today?" she asked, spearing the last bite of pancake.

"I noticed that your parents have a pontoon boat. How about if we take it out?"

"Great idea. Maybe we should stop at a grocery store and get some food to take with us," she suggested.

Eyebrows raised, he said, "We just ate."

"I know, but we're going to want lunch later, and the refrigerator is empty."

"You're the boss."

So, after they paid the bill, they left the restaurant and went to a nearby grocery store. It was the first time she'd done something as mundane as grocery shopping with him, but she discovered that she liked it. One thing was certain, life with Connor would never be boring.

After they'd picked out pre-made sandwiches, potato chips (yes, she had an addiction), and drinks, they were back in the Jeep and heading home. *Home.* Funny, it wasn't her home or Connor's home, but it felt like home now that they were there together. The only thing missing was Ava.

"I met a little girl in the park last night, and her name was Ava," Julia said.

"Oh yeah?"

"She was about two years old, but she made me think of your Ava and what she might be like at that age."

"If she's anything like me, she'll probably be a handful."

"And gorgeous."

"Well, thank you," he said, grinning from ear to ear.

"You can't take all the credit for that," Julia reminded him.

"No, but she does look a lot like me, don't you think?"

"Yes, she does." And thank God for that. If she'd looked like a mini-Cam, that would have been even harder to take.

"Do you miss her?" Julia asked.

"You know what's crazy? A while ago, I didn't even know she existed, and now I can't imagine my life without her."

"I know exactly what you mean," she said. *Just like I can't imagine my life without you.*

Once they returned to the house and unloaded the groceries, Connor said, "One slight problem. I didn't bring swim trunks."

"Hmmm. I guess you'll just have to swim in your tighty-whities."

Eyes wide, he said, "No way in hell!"

"I'm teasing. Let me check in my parents' bedroom. My dad probably has some trunks in one of the dresser drawers."

She'd already started down the hall toward the master bedroom when she realized Connor wasn't behind her. Turning around, she saw him standing at the opposite end of the hall with his hands on his hips.

"What's wrong?"

"There's no way I'm putting my boys in your dad's trunks," he said firmly.

She couldn't help it. She burst out laughing and had to lean against the wall to stop from falling over.

"You think I'm kidding, don't you?"

She couldn't even form a reply she was laughing so hard.

"Would you do it? Would you put your goods into someone else's swimsuit?"

Holding onto her stomach with both hands, she said, "Stop. I'm going to pee my pants!"

"See. Right there. That's exactly why I'm not going to wear your dad's trunks!"

Sliding down to the floor, Julia tried to contain her laughter, but when she glanced up at his serious expression, it made her fall into hysterics again.

"Okay. That's it. Join me outside when you're done," he muttered and started to walk away.

"Connor, wait. You'll be more comfortable if you wear trunks, and if it makes you feel better, you can keep your underwear on underneath."

"Fine, but nobody hears about this, especially not my brothers."

"Got it," she said, trying not to laugh again. "Follow me."

She'd forgotten how impressive the master suite was until they stepped inside. A vaulted ceiling and a wall of windows facing the lake made the room look even larger than it was. Connor walked around, admiring the space, while she started opening dresser drawers.

"I'd love to own a place like this someday," he remarked as he peered out the window.

"Maybe you will."

"Nah. I doubt I'll be able to afford it."

He'd made other comments about her parents' money, so she knew it bothered him, but she wasn't sure why. Before, he'd seemed perfectly content with his ranch house in the woods, and it suited him. As much as she liked the lake house, it was much larger and more pretentious than was necessary for a family of three. But this was how her parents had chosen to spend their money. It didn't mean she wanted or expected the same thing for herself.

"Even if you could afford it, would you really want a place this big?" she asked.

"Probably not."

"Me neither. Don't get me wrong. I love it here, but I would be just as happy with something smaller."

Apparently, her words had done the trick because a slow smile spread across his handsome face and warmed her to the core. Now she could turn her attention back to finding some swim trunks.

A minute later, she said, "Looks like you have two choices: black with fish on them or a Hawaiian floral print." She held up the swimsuits and dangled them before him as if to entice him.

"Wow. Tough decision," he replied, acting like he was giving it some serious thought.

"Just pick one!"

"I guess I'll go with the fish."

"Okay. I'll wait outside while you change," she said and tossed him the trunks.

But he didn't catch them because he'd already started stripping out of his clothes.

"Connor…"

"What? It's nothing you haven't seen before."

And just like that, his pants hit the floor, and he was stepping out of them. He'd already whipped off his shirt, so he was standing there in nothing but his black boxer briefs instead of the tighty-whities she'd accused him of wearing.

The underwear hugged him just right, and she couldn't help but appreciate the view. The man was built, and he still had the power to steal her breath away. She let her eyes wander over his broad chest, his tight abs, and then further down to the sexy indentions at his hips. She lingered on his muscular thighs with their smattering of dark hair before raising her eyes to meet his.

He was smirking at her, the dirty rat. He knew full well what he was doing, and it wasn't fair. Since he'd been at the lake house, they hadn't done anything except hold hands, which wasn't their usual M.O. Under normal circumstances, they wouldn't have been able to keep their hands off each other, so this was a serious lesson in self-control—at least on her part.

"You keep looking at me like that, and we won't make it out to the boat," he warned, his voice gruff.

Darting her eyes downward, she saw evidence that his warning was valid. In the time she'd been staring, he'd sported a full-on erection that was threatening to poke a hole through his underwear.

"I'll just go get changed," Julia said, hooking her thumb over her shoulder.

"Good idea," he said and laughed as she hurried out of the room.

It wasn't that she didn't want to have sex with him. It was that she wanted to decide the when and the where. She didn't want him to think that he could just show up, whisk her off to bed, and all would be forgiven or their problems would disappear.

Once she was safely in her bedroom with the door closed, she dug out her swimsuit and quickly changed into it. Julia was long past the point of obsessing over every detail of her curvy body. Yes, she had some extra meat on her bones, and yes, she liked to eat. But she also exercised (although not as diligently as some people), and generally, she felt good about herself.

She felt even more confident when she rejoined Connor downstairs, and he let out a long, low whistle. Even though she wore a cover-up over her swimsuit, it was made of mesh, so he could see right through it. The way he looked at her, she might as well have been naked. His eyes skimmed over her, heating her blood as they went. At this rate, she wasn't going to be able to keep him at bay for long.

"You're gorgeous," he said, taking a step toward her.

She smiled her thanks. "We should probably get going. It looks like the clouds are starting to roll in. There could be rain coming." She was babbling, but she couldn't seem to stop herself. Using the two beach towels she'd brought downstairs as a shield, she added, "Why don't you grab the food?"

Even in her dad's swim trunks with the fish all over them, Connor looked hot. Bare-chested, aviators propped up in his spiky hair, he took the bags of food off the kitchen counter and followed her outside and down the paved path to the boat dock.

The sun was high in the sky, and there was a slight breeze, the temperature approaching eighty degrees. However, it being Michigan, the weather could change in a heartbeat, and there were several clouds gathering off in the distance.

"Do you want to drive, or do you want me to?" Julia asked. She'd grabbed the boat key off the hook hanging by the back door on their way out.

"We could take turns," he suggested.

"Okay. I'll start," Julia said, thinking it would give her something to do other than thinking about what she really wanted to do—him!

Connor hopped into the boat first and then gave her a hand in before settling into the seat beside the driver's seat.

Getting behind the wheel, Julia turned the key, and the boat started right up. A few minutes later, they had reached the middle of the lake, and a sense of calm fell over her. The wind blew her hair back, and the waves lapped against the boat, creating a gentle rocking motion. She peeked over at Connor and saw that he looked as relaxed as she was. His head was tipped back against the seat, his long legs were stretched out before him, and his mouth was curled up in a satisfied smile.

He hadn't looked this peaceful since Cam had come back into his life, and Julia was glad that she was there to share it with him.

After a few spins around the lake, Julia pulled into a cove and shut off the engine.

"Is it my turn to drive already?" he asked.

"I thought we could just hang out here for a while."

"Sounds good to me," he said.

Connor moved to the back of the boat and leaned over the side to trail his fingertips in the water while she removed her cover-up. When he stood back up and turned around, his eyes went wide.

She'd found some sunscreen in a compartment in the boat and was rubbing it into her skin when she felt his eyes upon her.

"Nothing you haven't seen before," she teased, borrowing his phrase from earlier.

"I've never seen you in a bathing suit before," he countered, stalking toward her.

Oh boy. There was nowhere to hide from him now. She couldn't even back up for fear of falling overboard.

"Connor…"

"Yeah?" He'd stopped right in front of her, and now he was caressing the sensitive skin between her neck and shoulder.

"We're not doing this here," she said, her voice not sounding as firm as she'd wanted it to.

"Your nipples say otherwise."

Glancing down, she saw the evidence for herself. Her nipples were standing at attention, their outline pronounced beneath the thin material of her bikini.

"They're not thinking clearly," she said and was met with his hearty laughter.

"Just one touch," he said, begging her with his eyes.

"Somebody could see." But her back was to the shoreline in a spot that was sheltered by tall trees, and he was blocking her front with his broad chest.

"Nobody's looking."

He was right. There were plenty of boats on the water, but none were near enough to see them clearly.

"Just one touch," she said, finally giving in.

She assumed he would touch her on the outside of the swimsuit, which was why she gasped when he pulled the material aside and swiped his thumb over her right nipple.

It felt like there was an invisible line from her nipple to her core, and all her nerve endings stood up and rejoiced at his touch.

He added his index finger to the mix and was gently plucking her nipple while studying her reaction at the same time.

"You said one touch," she said, her voice quivering.

"But I didn't say for how long."

"Connor."

"You want more, don't you? God knows I do. I can't be this close to you and not want to touch you."

He'd covered up her right breast, but now he was fondling her left one, which he'd uncovered without her even realizing it. The haze of lust was already settling over her, and she melted into his touch. Taking a step forward, she rubbed up against his erection, feeling the distinct outline of him through the swim trunks.

Suddenly, Connor pulled back.

"What's wrong?" she asked, looking at him with concern.

"I forgot I was wearing your dad's trunks. We have to go back before I…"

Giggling, she said, "Oh, right. You can drive."

There was no need to spell it out. They both wanted the same thing, and the urgency propelled them back to the lake house as fast as the pontoon boat would go.

Chapter 19

Once the boat was docked, they didn't waste any time. Connor took the grocery bags, and they hurried back up the path to the house. They stopped off in the kitchen just long enough to put the sandwiches in the refrigerator, and then Connor picked her up in his arms and carried her through to the living room.

"Where to?" he asked.

"Upstairs," she replied, her lips nuzzling his neck.

He kept her in his hold and took the stairs like they were nothing.

"Now where?"

"To the left, last door on the right."

He didn't set her down until they were inside, and then he immediately removed her dad's trunks and tossed them aside.

She smiled as he wrapped his arms around her and pulled her close before leaning down and capturing her mouth in a long, luxurious kiss.

"God, I missed you," he said afterward.

"I missed you too," she admitted.

He made quick work of removing her cover-up and tossed it over his shoulder, where it landed on top of her dresser, and then he paused to admire her for a moment.

"I want you to know something, Jules."

Placing her palms on his chest, she felt the pounding of his heart. She'd expected to already be naked by now, so she was surprised that he'd stopped to talk.

"This isn't just about sex to me. What we have…what I feel…"

"It's okay. We don't have to talk right now," she said, smoothing her hands down his arms, finding his hands, and entwining their fingers together.

"Just let me say this."

"Okay."

"It may have started out that way, but it…*you*…mean so much more to me now. I'm not very good at this, am I?'

She smiled, wanting to assure him that he was a lot better at it than he thought, but then he continued.

"When you took off on me, I thought…well, I realized how much I wanted you in my life. And I know I probably don't deserve you, but…"

"Stop saying that."

"But I would never purposely hurt you. I think we've got something really special here, and I'd like to see where it goes. That is, if you're willing to stick it out with me."

Julia was nodding, but he didn't seem to notice. He just kept on talking.

"And I know it won't be easy, especially with Cam and Ava in the picture, but I'm willing to give it my best shot if you will too."

"Yes, yes, yes," she said, giggling softly. "I've been nodding my head during your entire speech."

"Oh. You have?"

"Yes. And yes, I'm willing to 'stick it out' with you, as you so eloquently put it."

"I'm not very good with words," he said, scratching the back of his head.

"There's another way," she whispered.

His head snapped up.

"You can show me."

"Now, that, I'm good at."

Sliding his hands up her back, he untied her bikini strings, freeing her breasts from their confines. He then lifted the top over her head and tossed it over his shoulder, where it landed on top of her cover-up.

"How are you doing that?" she said, laughing.

"I have no idea," he said, his voice thick with desire.

Next, he dropped to his knees in front of her, tucked his fingers in the sides of her bikini bottoms, and slowly slid them down her legs.

Instead of tossing the bottoms over his shoulder, he pushed them aside and scooted in closer, his face lined up with her…

"Ohhhh," she moaned as his tongue flicked out to tease her. And then he did it again before looking up at her through hooded eyes.

"More?" he asked, his breath blowing over the spot that he'd just kissed.

"Yes, please."

Cupping her bottom firmly, he proceeded to lick, kiss, and nibble until she became so lightheaded she had to grip his shoulders for support.

"Connor."

But he didn't show any signs of stopping, and so she held on for the ride, and oh, what a ride it was. She moaned unabashedly, and somehow, her hands were now entangled in his hair, and she was pushing his head forward as far as it could go.

When he found the magic button, she exploded, releasing all her pent-up emotions in one long, ecstatic cry.

Her entire body had gone limp, so she was grateful when Connor picked her up and carried her to the bed. Her eyes clouded with desire, she watched as he quickly removed his boxer briefs. But when he crawled over her, he frowned.

"What's wrong?" she asked, confused.

"I don't have any condoms with me."

"None?"

"No. I came up here to talk to you, and I didn't want to assume that anything else would happen."

She smiled then, so wide that she knew her gums were showing, but she didn't care.

"And this is a good thing, why?" he asked.

Reaching her hands up, she cupped his face and pulled him down for a kiss. When she let go, she said, "I love that you came all this way just to talk to me."

"Yeah?"

"Um-hmm."

"Tell me more," he said, grinning down at her.

"I love that you weren't afraid to go to my parents' house when you wanted to find me."

"That would be parent—singular."

"Yes, but how did you know that my dad wouldn't be there?"

"I didn't."

"See. I love that you didn't let anything deter you from getting to me."

He traced her lips with a finger and gazed at her reverently.

"Nothing could have stopped me. I don't want to lose you, Julia. Right now, that's my biggest fear."

Trailing a finger down the middle of his chest, she said, "And I love that you just told me that."

"None of this solves the problem of not having a condom, however," he said as if to remind her of what they were in the middle of doing.

"No worries," she said and pushed on his chest to get him to roll onto his back. Of course, that was like trying to move a huge boulder; however, he understood what she was doing and helped out.

Kneeling over his hips, she said, "Lay back and relax."

He obliged, crossing his hands behind his head and watching as she took his erection in both hands and bent over him. After treating him like her favorite brand of popsicle, his body tightened, and his hands fisted in her hair.

"Damn, Julia. You're too good to me."

She stopped what she was doing just long enough to smile up at him before putting her mouth on him again, this time taking him in as far as she could before slowly releasing him.

She loved watching him like this—loved seeing him shed his tough-guy persona to indulge in the raw pleasure that she brought him. Up until recently, Connor had worked hard to keep his emotions in check, but recently, he'd started to open up. And she liked seeing this new side of him. Discovering that he had a daughter had softened his rough edges, and he seemed more willing to expose the emotional side of himself. He'd shared more with her in the past eight hours than he had since they'd been dating, and the weight she'd been carrying around for the past few days had lifted.

"Julia," he growled, breaking into her thoughts.

It was a warning cry, but she didn't heed it. Instead, she nodded, and Connor let go, holding her head in place while he ground out his pleasure. When he loosened his grip, she slid up his body and nestled into his side, resting one hand on his chest, where she could feel the comforting rhythm of his heartbeat.

"I might have to forget a condom more often," he said after a minute.

She smiled against his skin before she remembered what Cam had said about them not always using protection. For some reason, she felt compelled to ask him about it even though now might not be the best time.

"Connor?"

"Um-hmm."

"What Cam said about you two not using protection—I find that difficult to believe. I mean, you've always been so diligent about it with me." She tried to keep the accusation out of her voice, and she hoped she'd succeeded because he was quiet for what felt like a long time.

"Cam told me she was on the pill, and I believed her. But recently, she admitted that she'd gone off it in the last couple months of our relationship."

Julia bolted upright. "So, she tried to trap you?"

"I don't know that for sure, and regardless, she'd never admit it. She said she thought we'd be safe for a while after she stopped the pill."

Julia smelled a rat—a blonde-haired, blue-eyed, conniving rat! She wouldn't put it past Cam to try to get pregnant so she could keep Connor tied to her. What would have happened if he hadn't caught Cam canoodling with her boss? They might still be together—Cam, Connor, and Ava.

"Hey," he said, sitting up beside her. "It doesn't really matter anymore, does it? I made a mistake, and I've paid for it. Plus, I almost lost you in the process."

Julia shook her head vehemently.

"You disagree?"

"You can't view Ava as a mistake. She's lovely, and she's yours. If she was a mistake, she's the sweetest mistake there ever was."

Leaning forward, he gently kissed her lips. "You know what? You're right. From now on, that's how I'm going to think of it."

"Just don't ever tell her that," Julia said solemnly. "Nobody wants to think they were a mistake."

Taking her hand in his, he kissed the back of it. "Hopefully, you'll always be around to remind me." And before she could respond, he tumbled back on the bed, taking her down with him.

An hour later, they were in the kitchen eating the sandwiches and potato chips they'd bought earlier.

"I need to leave early tomorrow morning," Connor said in between bites of his Italian sub.

"I figured."

"Finn will have my ass if I keep missing work like this. Especially now, when it's so busy."

"I'll probably head back too, even though Harper won't expect me at work for a couple days." Plus, now that she and Connor had reconciled, there was no reason to stay away. Maybe they could come back again during the summer under better circumstances, which gave her an idea...

"Hey. Maybe we could bring Ava up here sometime. Just the three of us for a weekend."

Connor smiled, a dollop of dressing on his lower lip that Julia wanted to lick off. "That's a great idea as long as Cam agrees."

At least this time, she didn't wince when he said Cam's name. Progress. "Why wouldn't she? She's your child too."

"I know, but I still have to respect Cam's feelings, Jules."

"I understand." But she didn't try to hide her disappointment. It sucked that they'd have to check with Cam whenever they wanted to spend time with Ava.

Reaching across the table, Connor rubbed his thumb across her cheek. "Maybe we could start smaller and work up to it. What do you say?"

"Sure." *Because what other choice do I have?*

The rest of the evening was pure bliss. After they finished eating, they spent the next two hours lounging on the deck, sitting side by side, holding hands, and talking.

"When we get home, I'm going to have a talk with Cam," Connor said, looking out over the lake.

"Sounds scary."

He chuckled. "I want to make it clear to her that there's no chance of us getting back together. I'm not going to let her manipulate me anymore."

Julia gave his hand a squeeze. "And I'm going to have a heart-to-heart with my dad. He needs to stop trying to reunite Alec and me and acknowledge that I'm with you now."

"Sounds like we have our work cut out for us."

"Where there's a will, there's a way." *Oh God. Now I sound like a cross-stitch saying!*

"At least we have a few people on our side."

"You mean Harper and Finn?"

"And Liam and my parents."

Suddenly, it struck her that her parents still hadn't met Ava. She was going to have to fix that too. Maybe if they saw her with Connor and his daughter, her parents would start to accept that she was serious about him.

They stayed outside until the sun began to descend, and then Connor stood up and held out his hand.

"Where are we going?" she asked, searching his eyes for clues.

"Back inside. This might be the last night we have alone for a while, and I want to make the most of it."

Smiling big, she said, "I couldn't agree more."

Chapter 20

Connor hadn't realized how much he'd missed his daughter until he held her in his arms again. Her chubby little hands and feet flailed with glee at the sight of him, and he melted. How was it possible for such a little person to have such a big effect on him?

"I think she missed you," Cam said from where she sat on his couch. "And I did too."

Uh-oh. Her admission didn't bode well for the conversation he was about to have with her.

Still holding Ava, he sat down on the chair opposite of Cam and prepared for battle. He handed Ava a teething ring and bounced her on his knee as he tried to figure out where to start. But Cam beat him to it.

"I have good news. While you were gone, an apartment opened up in the building we looked at. I'm going to move in next week."

"That is good news."

"And it's only a mile from here, so you can visit me and Ava anytime."

"I don't just want to visit her, Cam. I want Ava to stay with me some of the time too."

"Of course," she said, waving her hand around like it was a given. "Will you help me move in when

192

it's time? The unit is on the third floor, so I'll need help carrying things up the stairs."

"Sure. My brothers can help too if we need the extra muscle."

"Your muscles are more than enough," she said flirtatiously.

Okay, maybe Julia was right. Maybe Cam did want him back. Just then, Ava dropped her teething ring, and a plop of drool landed on his jeans.

"Is she okay? Why is she so *wet?*" he asked.

Cam laughed. "Yes, she's fine. All babies drool, especially when they're cutting teeth."

"Sounds painful."

"It makes her fussy at times, but if she has something to chew on, she's usually okay."

Handing the teething ring back to Ava, he tried to remember where they'd left off. Who knew babies could be so distracting?

"Where were we?"

"We were talking about your muscles," Cam said with a wink. And then she purposefully crossed her legs, giving Connor a view up her skirt.

Averting his eyes, he said, "Don't."

"Don't what?" she asked.

"Don't flirt with me. It won't work."

"It used to."

"That was a long time ago."

"Back when you used to love me."

"*Used to* being the operative phrase."

"Oh, come on, Connor. You can't possibly feel that way about Gillian."

He glared at her. "Julia. Don't pretend you don't know her name."

"Whatever. The point is, you loved me once, and now we have a child together. We could be a family."

"No, Cam. We can't."

And then, as if Ava sensed the discord between her parents, she started to fuss.

"I think she needs to eat," Cam said, standing and holding out her arms.

"I'll hold her while you get the bottle," Connor said, standing his ground. He didn't want Cam thinking he was incapable of caring for Ava. That wouldn't help his cause any.

Cam huffed out of the room to warm a bottle while Connor stood up and started pacing. Bouncing Ava up and down in his arms, he willed her to stop fussing, but it was to no avail. The second Cam reappeared with a bottle, Ava calmed down, and Cam went to take her from him again.

"I'll do it," he said, snatching the bottle from her hand before she could argue.

Sitting back down, he cradled Ava against his chest and offered her the bottle. He watched with something akin to awe as she suckled and stared back at him. It was almost as if she were trying to memorize his features—features that looked a lot like hers. It was amazing, really, and for a moment, he forgot that Cam was even there.

"You're getting better at it," Cam said softly.

It was the first compliment she'd given him that hadn't made him uncomfortable. "I'm trying."

Tucking her bare feet underneath her, she smoothed her skirt over her legs, but this time, she didn't give him a peep show. Maybe she was finally taking the hint. But just in case...

"Look, Cam. I know this has been hard for you, and believe me, I have a better appreciation for single moms than ever before. But I'm here to help in any way I can, and I think I've proven that."

She nodded, her fingers clasped tightly in her lap.

"But you and I are never going to be together. I'm with Julia now."

"Do you love her?" Cam asked as if she were issuing him a challenge.

He swallowed hard. He hadn't put his feelings for Julia into those exact words, but he was getting closer to that. However, he didn't want Cam to be the first to know.

"I didn't think so," she said, looking victorious.

"What I feel for Julia is between her and me. My relationship with her is private."

"If she's going to be spending time with my daughter, I have a right to ask questions."

His eyes went wide. "*Your* daughter? I believe she belongs to both of us."

"You weren't even there for the first few months of her life."

"And whose fault was that?"

Okay. Breathe, Connor. This was not going well at all. He decided to try a different tact.

"What about you? What happened with Tyler?"

Flapping her manicured hand around, she said, "That was nothing. It ended a long time ago."

Just then, Ava's mouth went slack, and formula started dribbling down the side of her face.

"She needs to be burped," Cam said, darting across the room with a burp cloth in hand.

After wiping off Ava's face, he flung the cloth over his shoulder, hoisted her up, and gently patted her back until she emitted a puff of air. After a few more pats, she emitted a much louder burp, which made him and Cam laugh.

"Yep. She definitely takes after me," he said.

"I won't argue there," Cam said, smiling for the first time in the last several minutes.

See, he wanted to say. *We'll get along fine if we just keep it about Ava.*

"So, we were talking about Tyler."

"No, you were talking about Tyler," she corrected.

"Is there any chance for you two?"

"Not unless he divorces his wife, which I don't see happening anytime soon."

"Well, is there someone else you're interested in? Someone from work maybe?"

Cam laughed, but it wasn't joyful. "I see what you're trying to do, Connor, but there's no one else right now. There aren't too many men out there who want to be saddled down with a single mom and child."

Connor immediately thought about Julia, who'd agreed to stick by him even though he was a single dad. Everyone deserved someone like that in their life, even Cam.

"What do you see in her, anyway? She doesn't seem like your type," Cam said, breaking into his thoughts.

Ignoring her tone, he twisted his neck to peek at Ava, who had fallen asleep on his shoulder. While he was enjoying her soft, warm body next to his, he decided it was time to set her down and focus on Cam.

He wanted to get this conversation over with and get on to more important things—like Julia.

Careful not to jostle her too much, he walked across the room and laid Ava in the bouncy seat. He was already beginning to understand the importance of naptime, and he hoped that she would stay sleeping long enough for him to accomplish what he'd set out to do.

Instead of returning to the chair, he sat next to Cam on the couch, leaving ample space between them. Maybe if he could convince her that they were a team in raising their child, she would loosen up about Julia. It was his only hope.

"Julia's warm, and funny, and kind. I care about her—a lot. But that doesn't mean that I don't have room in my life for Ava, and for you too as Ava's mother. I only want what's best for both of you." There. Maybe he was getting better with words, after all.

"What if you're what's best for me?" Cam said. Her voice had softened, and he thought he saw a tear in her eye.

He shook his head. "I don't think you really believe that. I think you're just scared to be alone, even though you're not. Besides me, there are a lot of other people who are willing to help with Ava." *Including Julia*, he thought but didn't say.

She didn't argue with him that time, but she averted her eyes and picked at a loose thread on her skirt. "I really screwed up, didn't I?' she said, her voice sounding small and very far away.

"You can't think like that," Connor said, placing his hand over hers.

"I've made so many mistakes." A tear dripped down her cheek, but he resisted the urge to wipe it away.

"We all make mistakes," he said quietly, "but Ava isn't one of them."

Looking across the room, he saw that Ava was still sleeping, her head cocked to one side and her lips moving as if she were still sucking on the bottle. She was so darn adorable that it made his heart squeeze.

"I'm so sorry, Connor. I never got a chance to tell you that. I've always regretted hurting you, but I'll never regret loving you."

He nodded, his throat tight with emotion. *What's happening to me? Why am I becoming a wuss?*

Their conversation having come to a natural end, Cam got ready to leave. Connor helped transfer Ava into the car seat, and then he went back inside to a house that suddenly felt very empty. He could still detect the lingering scent of Ava in the air—a combination of sweet baby skin and formula.

Flopping down on the chair, he accidentally sat on her teething ring, and he pulled the soggy toy out from under him. Twisting it around in his hand, he smiled, remembering what Julia had said at the lake house about Ava being the sweetest mistake.

He'd tried to get that point across to Cam and hoped that he'd succeeded. And then he flicked on the television because all this emotional stuff was exhausting! As he was channel surfing, he decided that he needed a night out with the guys—his brothers in particular. He needed to feel like a man again instead of a wuss. Having made the decision to call them and set something up, he relaxed into the recliner and let his mind drift.

He thought about Ava, his conversation with Cam, and Julia. He would have called her right after Cam left, but she was with her parents. They'd decided to tackle their two biggest obstacles right after they'd returned from Up North. He still couldn't quite believe all that had happened to him in such a short amount of time.

First Julia and then Ava, both of whom had him wrapped around their little fingers. He smiled then, realizing there was no place else he'd rather be.

Chapter 21

It was one of only two times that Julia felt uncomfortable in her childhood home. The first was when she'd brought Connor over for dinner, and the second was now, as she faced her parents across the dining room table. Even the aroma of homemade chocolate cake didn't make her feel better.

"Did you enjoy your stay at the lake house?" Dr. Lee asked.

"Not completely." She'd been trying to decide how to begin, and he'd just given her an opening.

"Oh? Why not?"

"Well, I was having a fine time until Alec showed up."

Debra looked down and shifted the vegetables around on her plate.

"Ah," her dad said.

And then, because she was horrible at subtlety, Julia blurted out, "You have to let it go, Dad. Alec and I are *not* getting back together."

Her dad looked startled for a moment, but then he gave her a slight nod.

"I'm with Connor now, and I know you don't particularly like him…"

"Now, hold it right there."

Uh-oh. It wasn't very often that her dad took that tone with her. "I never said I didn't like him."

"You didn't have to. It was written all over your face the first time you met him."

He sighed. "I'm sorry, Julia, but he doesn't seem like your type."

She tucked her hands beneath her thighs to keep them from banging the table. "Who is my type? A doctor like you and Alec?"

"Now, honey," Debra said in an attempt to calm her down. But Julia was on a roll.

"Connor may not be a doctor, or a lawyer, or whatever else you deem to be a suitable occupation, but he's excellent at what he does, and his business is very successful."

"I thought it was his brother's business," Dr. Lee said.

"He and his brothers are equal partners, and eventually, Connor wants to branch off on his own."

"That's all well and good, but does he have the means to take care of you in the manner to which you're accustomed?"

She'd never thought of her dad as snobby until right then, and it pained her. Looking over at her mom for help, she saw that she was on her own. Her mom belonged to a different generation. She'd been content in her role as a wife and mother and well taken care of by her doctor husband. But Julia wasn't like that. She didn't need anyone to take care of her or provide things for her. She was capable of doing that all by herself. She wasn't with Connor for what he could give her. She was with him because...

"I love him," she said quietly, testing out the words. And they felt right. "I love him," she repeated more emphatically.

"Love doesn't pay the bills," Dr. Lee said.

"Now, James," her mother said, finally breaking her silence. "Listen to your daughter. She's in love with Connor, and we should be happy for her. She's not a child anymore."

Her dad stared at Debra for a moment in shock, but when he turned and saw the tears streaming down Julia's face, he visibly softened.

"And you're okay with taking on another woman's child?" he asked.

Swiping away her tears, Julia said, "Ava's his child too, and I love her. I'd like you both to meet her." She'd sidestepped his question because she wasn't sure how to answer, but she'd been truthful about her feelings for Ava. And she truly believed that once her parents met Ava, they'd fall in love with her too, regardless of who her mother was.

"Okay, then," Dr. Lee said. "I'll have to trust your judgment."

It wasn't overly encouraging, but it was a step in the right direction. Debra rubbed Julia's back a few times and then stood up to serve dessert.

Julia excused herself to the bathroom, where she splashed cool water on her tear-stained face and took some deep breaths. She'd done it. She'd stood up to her father and proclaimed her love for Connor all in one swoop.

But now she suffered a brief moment of uncertainty. Did Connor feel the same way about her? He'd been so sweet and attentive to her at the lake house, and he'd shared more of himself than he had up until then. He'd told her how much he cared about her and how important she was, but was that the same as love?

There were still a lot of unknowns, and she dealt better with certainties. Case in point: her career choice, where one plus one always added up to two. Thinking back, it was probably the same reason that she'd been with Alec. He was known to her, and he was calm, steady, and predictable. He would have given her the kind of life her father had alluded to—a life of comfort and luxury.

But in the end, that hadn't been enough. She hadn't loved Alec passionately the way she did Connor. She probably would have ended up bored and childless. And now look, Connor had suddenly become part of a package deal. If they stayed together, she'd have Ava too, and hopefully more children down the road.

Hold on, Julia. You're getting way ahead of yourself.

When she returned to the dining room, her dad was no longer at the table, but there were three thick slices of chocolate cake at each of their seats.

"Where'd Dad go?" Julia asked as she sat back down.

"He had to take a phone call," Debra said.

After taking her first bite of the moist cake, Julia said, "Thanks, Mom."

"I know it's your favorite," she said.

"Not just for the cake. For sticking up for me in front of Dad."

Debra patted her hand. "You know he means well, right? You're our only child, and he worries about you. We both do. Once you have your own child, you'll understand."

"I'm already starting to," Julia said, thinking about Ava.

Julia felt much lighter when she left her parents' house, and she wondered if Connor had had similar success with Cam. She considered driving straight to his house, but she didn't want to interrupt if they were still talking. She was still debating what to do when she pulled onto her street and saw his Jeep in her driveway. Apparently, he was anxious to see her too, and the thought of that made her heart swell.

When she pulled in beside him, she saw that his head was leaned back and his eyes were closed. Was he sleeping in her driveway? She made a mental note to give him a key to her house. And then his eyes popped open, and he smiled at her—a slow, sleepy grin that made her insides warm.

They both got out of their cars at the same time, and he lifted her right off her feet and spun her around.

Laughing, she said, "What was that for?"

"Just for fun," he said as he set her back down and followed her into the house.

Once they were behind closed doors, he pulled her into his arms and planted a firm kiss on her lips, making a loud smacking noise when he pulled away.

"Wow! Does this mean things went well with Cam?"

"As well as you might expect," he said, making himself at home on the couch.

She set down her purse and joined him, nestling in close and soaking up his presence. "Tell me everything."

"Ladies first. How did it go with Dr. Lee?"

There was no malice when he said her dad's title, and she decided that he was just being respectful. So, she launched into a summary of her conversation with her parents and ended it on what she hoped was a positive note.

Afterward, she said, "Now tell me about your discussion with Cam."

He gave her the highlights, shifting uncomfortably when he confirmed her suspicions about Cam still wanting to be with him. But Julia didn't have the heart to say, "I told you so," especially when she thought about how difficult the conversation must have been for him. It sounded like he'd said all the right things without giving Cam any false hopes. There was a part of Julia that felt sorry for Cam. She'd messed up a good thing, and they were all in an awkward situation because of it. On the other hand, Julia wouldn't have been with Connor if things hadn't gone the way they did.

"It sounds like you handled it well," she said.

"I did my best. Oh, and there's one more thing I wanted to tell you."

He'd raised his right arm to run his hand through his hair, and she caught a glimpse of his tattoo. Crazy enough, just the sight of it turned her on. She had the sudden urge to touch it, to touch him, but he wasn't done talking yet.

"I scheduled a guys' night out for next Saturday. I hope you don't mind."

Eyebrows raised, she said, "Why would I mind?"

"I don't know. I just don't want you to think I'm ditching you on a Saturday night."

She laughed. "Connor, I'm perfectly capable of entertaining myself."

His eyes widened. "I just got an amazing visual."

"That's not what I meant!"

"I was kidding, but not really. I liked watching you that time. I still replay it in my head."

She squirmed even though she was secretly pleased. She liked that he was just as turned on by her as she was by him.

"It can happen again, ya know."

He perked up. "Oh yeah? Like when?"

Shooting him a seductive smile, she stood and offered her hand. "How about right now?"

"Hell yeah," he said and jumped off the couch.

By the time they got to her bedroom, he already had his shirt off and was unbuttoning his jeans.

"In a hurry much?" she teased.

"I'm not in a hurry, I'm anxious. There's a difference," he said as his pants hit the floor.

"I'm anxious too," she said as she whipped her T-shirt off and tossed it aside.

Her bra went next, and her nipples stood at attention under his intense gaze.

"Damn, woman!"

He sucked in a breath when she stepped out of her jeans and panties, and she noticed he still hadn't removed his boxers.

Crawling onto the bed, she propped herself up with pillows and leaned back so she could still see him. "I guess I'll have to get started without you," she said. Who knew she had a temptress inside her? Knowing she was safe with Connor, she felt free to let go of her inhibitions and explore, and his reactions spurred her on.

Raising her hands to her chest, she cupped her breasts, feeling their weight before brushing her fingers over her taut nipples. Smiling, he watched her and started to remove his boxers, his erection springing forth just as her right hand disappeared between her legs.

Swallowing hard, his Adam's apple bobbing in his throat, he said, "Are you wet for me?"

His voice sounded deeper in the dim light of her bedroom, and her breath quickened.

"Yes," she said.

"Good. Keep going while I get a condom. I remembered this time."

"Thank God," she said as she grazed her fingers over her tight bud.

Keeping his eyes on her movements, he quickly sheathed himself, but he didn't move until she beckoned him forward. Her body was on fire, and while she hadn't minded starting without him, she wanted him to take her to the finish line.

Crawling over her, he pulled her hand away and replaced it with his erection. "My turn," he growled.

"Ohhhhh," she moaned as he pushed inside, their bodies molding together perfectly.

Once he was buried deep, he lowered his head to capture her lips. The man was an expert kisser. First, he sucked her full bottom lip between his, the pressure causing the slightest bit of pain before he released it and ran his tongue across it.

"Connor," she said, wriggling her hips beneath him.

"Good?"

"Yes."

Next, he plundered her mouth with his tongue while gripping her left hip at the same time and thrusting into her.

Her brain shut down, and all she could do was feel. Her nipples rubbing against his chest, her core tightening, her legs wrapping around his powerful thighs as he plunged into her. With the friction building, her breath came in short gasps, and she knew she was getting close.

"Julia," he said, panting against her mouth.

With her name on his lips, they came in a powerful burst of energy, bodies slick with sweat, lips swollen, limbs shaking, hearts pounding.

Afterward, when Connor had cleaned up and rejoined her, he curled his body around hers and held her tight.

Gathering her long hair in one hand, he moved it to the side so he could nuzzle her neck, causing her to shiver.

"Cold?" he said.

"No. It's just you."

"Me?"

"Yeah. You do that to me."

She felt his smile against her neck.

"You do that to me too," he said.

She smiled too even though she was facing away from him and he couldn't see it. "Stay with me tonight," she whispered.

"I'm not going anywhere."

"Me either."

"I would hope not since this is your house."

She laughed. "This is good, isn't it? This thing between us," she said, her throat tight with emotion.

"Not just good. The best."

Twisting to look at him over her shoulder, she said, "Ever?"

"Ever."

He hadn't said he loved her, but she felt loved, more so with each passing day. Their relationship wasn't perfect, and it wasn't easy, but it was everything she needed and then some.

Chapter 22

"This is so much fun. Thanks for asking me to come," Megan said.

"It is fun. I haven't had a night out with the girls in a long time. Not since I've been dating Finn," Harper said.

"You guys need to get out more," Harper's sister, McKayla, said drily.

Julia laughed. "I guess you're the only truly single one among us." But she said it without envy. She was happy to be "off the market" now that she was with Connor.

"Another round?" Their waiter had approached the table, and they'd been so busy chatting they hadn't noticed.

"Sure! Why not?" Harper said, answering for all of them.

"This is going to be my last drink," Megan said, "since I'm the designated driver."

After Connor had told her about his guys' night out, Julia had arranged a girls' night out for the same evening. Looking around the table at her friends, she was glad she had. It was nice to have other women to share things with, and with these three women, she didn't have to hold back.

"So, how are things going with you and Connor?" Megan asked.

"I thought we weren't going to talk about men tonight," McKayla huffed.

Harper scowled at her. "Talking about men is what girls' night is all about! We have to dish about our men—it's a requirement."

McKayla rolled her eyes and took a sip of wine.

"In answer to your question, things are going pretty good considering his ex-girlfriend is in the picture," Julia said.

"How do you handle that one?" Megan said.

"Very carefully," Julia replied.

"She's a rock star," Harper said, rubbing Julia's arm encouragingly. "Only a strong woman could deal with it the way she has."

"He's worth it," Julia said, smiling unabashedly.

Harper gave her a knowing look, and Megan smiled.

"Why are you two so hung up on those O'Brien brothers, anyway?" McKayla asked.

They all gaped at her.

"Are you kidding? If I wasn't engaged to Will, I'd have been all over those boys," Megan said.

And now they all gaped at Megan, who, up until then, had seemed like the most conservative one of the bunch.

"What? They're gorgeous. I'd have to be dead not to notice. Of course, I'm very happy with Will," she added, perhaps for Julia's benefit. He was Julia's cousin, after all.

"Will's a great guy," Harper said, smiling at Megan. Harper and Will had dated for a short time, but if Megan was jealous, she never let it show.

"How about a toast?" Megan said, holding up her wine glass. "To all the wonderful men in our lives!"

Harper and Julia immediately held up their glasses. The only holdout was McKayla, who was tracing a finger around the rim of her glass like she hadn't heard a word they'd said.

"Kay, aren't you going to toast with us?" Harper asked, eyeing her curiously.

"I can't. I don't have a wonderful man to toast to. But you guys go ahead."

The three of them clinked glasses and took a drink, but Harper continued to study her sister over the rim of her glass.

"What happened to that guy you were dating recently? What was his name again?" Harper asked.

"Dylan?"

"Right. What happened to him?"

"We went out a few times, but it was no big deal. I haven't heard from him in a while."

"What about Liam?" Julia said.

McKayla's hand tightened around the stem of her glass. "What about him?"

Uh-oh. Connor had told Julia that Liam was interested in McKayla, but why was she acting surprised? *Me and my big mouth!*

"I just thought..." Julia began, but Harper interrupted.

"C'mon, Kay. It's no secret that Liam's interested in you."

McKayla shrugged. "Doesn't matter because I'm not interested in him."

Megan cleared her throat noisily, and they all turned to look at her. "I was just going to say that he's the last available O'Brien brother..."

"It's not going to happen," McKayla insisted.

"Why not?" Julia asked.

"Because, one, we work together, and two, we have nothing in common *except* that we work together. And everybody knows it's not a good idea to mix business with pleasure."

Harper smiled like she was proud of her. "McKayla's learned that lesson the hard way."

"Let's not talk about me," McKayla said. "Let's go back to talking about your men."

Since Julia had brought up Liam to begin with, she decided it was her duty to change the subject.

"Tell us more about your wedding plans, Meg," Julia said.

"Sure. But can we order some food first? This wine is going straight to my head!"

Harper flagged down the waiter, and they placed their food orders before they resumed talking.

"So, we decided where we're going to have the wedding," Megan said. She waited for a dramatic pause and then said, "Jekyll Island, Georgia!"

McKayla gave her a blank stare. "Never heard of it."

Harper scowled at her sister. "I've heard of it, although I've never been there. Sounds romantic."

"Makes me think of Dr. Jekyll and Mr. Hyde," McKayla said, and they all giggled.

"I've never been there either, but I've seen pictures. It looks beautiful," Julia said.

"A lot of my relatives live down South, so we thought that might be a good location," Megan explained. "I went there once when I was a kid, and I have great memories of it. We still haven't set the exact date, but we're working on it."

"Well, I vote for a winter wedding. That way, we can escape the snow for a while," Julia said.

"Even though it's not *our* decision, I'm with Jules. It would be great to go to a warmer climate during the winter," Harper said.

McKayla hadn't said anything, and Julia figured it was because she wasn't invited to the wedding. This was the first time she and Megan had met, so it made sense. But part of her thought it would be fun if McKayla and Liam could be there too. *Who knows? Maybe they'll be a couple by then.*

When the waiter arrived with the food and set their plates in front of them, Julia noticed that he took an extra-long look at McKayla. And who could blame him? She was a striking woman with her flippy light-blonde hair and large hazel eyes. You could tell that she and Harper were sisters; however, McKayla had a style all her own—sort of Bohemian meets girl next door. She wore very little makeup, but her skin glowed, and she had a natural beauty that really stood out. She was even prettier when she smiled, which didn't occur very often. According to Harper, McKayla had a history of failed relationships, and she'd had a hard time holding down a job. Harper, the quintessential older sister, had stepped in and asked Finn to hire her at O'Brien Brothers Landscaping, and so far, McKayla seemed to be working out fine.

McKayla was obviously trying to get her life back on track, which was probably why she hadn't responded to Liam's advances. As she'd said, "Business and pleasure don't mix."

"Are you ladies celebrating anything special tonight?" the waiter asked after he'd topped off their water glasses.

He looked at McKayla again, but she'd already dug into her meal and wasn't paying attention.

"No. Just a ladies' night out," Julia replied. The waiter had been very attentive all night long, and now she knew why. He had his sights set on McKayla.

"Just four single ladies out on the town, huh?" the waiter said not so subtly.

"Actually, only one of us is single," Megan replied. And then she smiled and pointed at McKayla.

McKayla's head popped up, her pasta wrapped around her fork and poised at her mouth. "Yep. That would be me," she said and waved her free hand at the waiter before sticking the fork in her mouth.

Julia eyed the waiter more closely and thought that he looked several years younger than them and might even be a college student. But he was good looking in a messy-haired, stubbled-jaw, nerdy sort of way. Not as hot as Connor, but still. And now McKayla was eyeing him a little more closely too.

"I'll be back to check on you ladies. Enjoy your meals," the waiter said and sauntered away.

McKayla stared after him, and Harper nudged her shoulder.

"You were staring at his butt," Harper accused, feigning disgust.

Julia and Megan snickered.

"Why shouldn't I? I'm the only single one here, remember?" McKayla said.

"Which brings up a good question," Megan said, setting down her fork. "Butts, abs, arms, or legs? Which do you ladies prefer?"

Julia's eyes popped out, and Harper choked on her hamburger.

"What? It's ladies' night!" Megan said a little too loudly.

"Yeah, and I think you just forfeited your job as designated driver," McKayla said.

Her comment set off a round of laughter, and suddenly, they were being stared at by several people at the surrounding tables.

"Do you ladies need anything else?" They hadn't even noticed the waiter reappear, and his question made them laugh even louder.

"No. We're good," McKayla said with a wink.

After he'd walked away, Megan said, "You haven't answered my question."

"Ah, what the hell! I'm all about the abs. I especially love it when Finn works outside without his shirt," Harper said, wiggling her eyebrows.

McKayla made a fake barfing sound.

"I'm an arms girl," Julia said. "I love Connor's muscular arms, especially the one with the tattoo on it."

"That is pretty hot," Harper said before sticking a french fry in her mouth.

"Hey. You have your own O'Brien brother," Julia teased.

"What about you, Megan? You have to answer too," Harper said.

"I thought the person who asked the question was exempt," Megan said, her cheeks turning pink.

Julia wasn't sure if it was from the wine or from their talk, but Megan had started it.

"Come on, Meg. Spill.," Julia said.

"It's kind of weird since Will is your cousin," said Megan, shifting in her seat.

"I'll just pretend you're talking about someone else," Julia said.

"This is going to sound really stupid," Megan said, twisting her napkin nervously.

"Just tell us," McKayla said.

"His ears," she whispered.

"What?" Julia said, cupping her ear and leaning forward. The restaurant had become a lot louder since they'd arrived, and she'd had trouble hearing Megan.

"Yes. That's exactly it," McKayla said, pointing to Julia's ear.

"His *ears*?" Julia said.

Harper was trying to hide her laughter behind her napkin but was failing miserably.

"See? I told you it sounds stupid," Meg said.

"It's not stupid. Tell us what you like about his ears," McKayla said, looking genuinely interested.

Julia wondered how McKayla was keeping a straight face, when she wanted to burst out laughing along with Harper.

"They're just so soft, and they're the perfect size, and I like to nibble on them when we're…" Megan's voice trailed off at the stricken look on Julia's face.

"Enough!" Julia cried. "I can't take anymore!"

Megan took a long drink from her water glass, looking like she regretted starting this conversation in the first place.

"Wait a minute. McKayla hasn't answered yet," Harper said.

All eyes shifted to McKayla, who had just taken another large bite of pasta.

So far, Julia had only seen her eat bread and pasta, and she wondered how the woman could stay so trim.

After she swallowed, McKayla said very loudly and clearly, "I like butts—nice, firm, perfectly shaped butts!"

The waiter had chosen that moment to walk up to their table. The expression on his face indicated that he'd heard McKayla's proclamation, and they all waited for his reaction.

"Butts, huh? I've been told I have a decent one."

With that, they broke into raucous laughter except for McKayla, who said, "I'll be the judge of that." And then she motioned for him to turn around.

Harper started to slink down in her chair, and Megan buried her face in her napkin while Julia looked on with amusement. McKayla had sass, that was for sure, and Julia liked her more by the minute.

Seemingly thrilled to be asked, the waiter did a slow turn, even going so far as to lift up his black apron and wiggle his butt for them. When he turned back around, he said, "Well, what's the verdict?"

But before McKayla could reply, a group of men approached their table—a group of tall, attractive men, three of whom looked strikingly similar.

The women froze, and one of the men tapped the waiter on the shoulder.

"Excuse me, but are these ladies bothering you?"

"Um, no, sir. They're just having a little fun, that's all," the waiter said, looking dwarfed by the other men.

"Well, we could hear them laughing all the way across the room, and since we know these ladies personally, we'd be happy to escort them out if you need us to."

"Connor!" Julia said, torn between being irritated and happy to see him. They hadn't discussed where they were going that evening, and she found it ironic that they'd ended up at the same place. Of course, Brandon wasn't that big a town.

"That's right. We'd be happy to throw them over our shoulders and carry them out of here," Finn said, smiling at Harper.

Liam just stood there and stared at McKayla while Will moved around the table and clapped a hand on his fiancé's shoulder.

"Of course, my bride-to-be is completely innocent here, right?" Will said, grinning down at Megan, whose cheeks had turned bright red.

"Um, I have another table to tend to," the waiter said and scurried away.

"Now look what you guys did! You scared him off," McKayla whined.

"Were you looking at his *butt*?" Liam said, a somewhat bemused expression on his face.

"So what if I was? I'm the only single one at this table," she stated firmly.

Julia and everyone else watched their interaction closely, but nobody dared interfere.

"I'm glad to see you ladies are having fun," Connor teased.

"Yes, and I'm sure you guys have been having fun too," Julia replied, her eyes sparkling. Connor looked exceptionally gorgeous, and suddenly, she was ready for ladies' night to be over with, but she wouldn't abandon her girls.

"Well, we'll leave you to it," Finn said, and bending down, he gave Harper a quick kiss on the lips.

"Yes, and if you need a ride home, let us know," Will said, ever the responsible one. "I'm the designated driver in our group, and we have plenty of room for four more."

"We're fine," Megan said. "Just having a little fun."

Leaning down, Connor whispered in Julia's ear, "Be safe," and then he gently kissed her cheek before wandering away with Finn and Will.

That left Liam, who was still standing there, seemingly rooted in place.

"I can't believe you were harassing the waiter like that," he said to McKayla, arms crossed over his muscular chest.

"Why not? He's young and good looking, and besides, it's really none of your business," she hissed.

"Okay, you two, back to your corners," Harper said, eyes darting from one to the other.

Sighing, Liam threw up his hands and walked away while McKayla watched him go. Everybody noticed but nobody said a word when they saw her staring straight at his butt!

Chapter 23

Once the guys were back at their table, they started on their third round of beers. Well, except for Will, who had switched to water since he was the designated driver.

"Man, our ladies are hot!" Finn said, pretending to wipe the sweat off his brow.

"You can say that again," Connor chimed in. Having heard Julia's laughter from across the room, he'd immediately gone in search of it, and the other guys had eagerly followed. None of them had known that they'd end up at the same place as their girlfriends, but none of them seemed to mind (except for Liam, who was scowling into his beer glass).

"What's wrong, man?" Connor asked, even though he had a pretty good idea what the problem was, or who in this case.

"Not a thing," Liam said, keeping his eyes trained on his glass.

"Don't mind him. He just hasn't gotten laid in a while," Finn teased.

"I can tell I'm out with the guys," Will said thoughtfully.

"How's that?" asked Finn.

"Because with Megan, we talk about 'making love' not 'getting laid.'"

They all chuckled, even Liam.

"So, when are you going to ask her out?" Finn said, eyeballing his youngest brother.

"Who?" Liam said.

"You know who," Connor said.

"Are we talking about McKayla?" Will asked innocently.

Liam's head jerked up, and the answer was written all over his face.

"Bingo!" Finn said.

"She's a pretty lady just like her sister," Will said. Everyone stilled for a moment, and Connor noticed Finn's hand tighten around his beer glass. Everyone at the table knew that Harper had dated Will for a short time before she'd gotten together with Finn. That was months ago, but Finn obviously still felt jealous over it.

To his credit, Finn replied, "Harper's the most beautiful woman there is to me."

Liam had been sitting there quietly until Connor nudged him. "So, what's it going to be, bro? Are you going to grow a set and ask her out?"

"I have asked, okay? She turned me down."

Pretending like he hadn't already known this, Connor said, "So, the O'Brien brothers' charm isn't working, huh?"

Liam shrugged. "Not yet, but I'll keep trying."

"That's the spirit," Will said. And then, holding up his water glass, he said, "How about a toast to the beautiful women we love and who love us back?"

Love? Really? Just the thought of it made Connor's heart race. The word had slipped off Will's tongue smooth as silk, but he was getting married soon, so it made sense. Finn and Harper had recently moved in together, and Connor suspected that they'd be next. That left him and Liam. But Liam had lowered his head and appeared to be busy choosing the best-looking mozzarella stick from the appetizer tray.

"C'mon, Connor. Raise your glass," Finn demanded.

Feeling ill at ease, Connor obeyed, and the three of them clinked glasses before taking a drink.

"Why the hesitation, man?" Finn asked once they'd set their drinks down.

Connor shrugged. "Julia and I haven't said that to each other yet." Maybe it was the beer that was making him talk, or maybe he just really needed some input from the guys, but he continued. "Things haven't exactly been smooth and easy for us."

Finn and Will laughed. "Love isn't supposed to be easy," Finn said.

"If it's too easy, it's probably friendship, not love," Will added.

Finn eyed him for a second as if he knew Will was referring to Harper.

"Hold on. Is this guys' night or ladies' night?" Liam asked. "Because right now, it sounds an awful lot like ladies talking."

"Don't be jealous, Lee," Finn said, giving him a little shove.

"Why would I be? I'm the only guy here who can go out with whoever he wants."

Connor laughed. "There's only one woman you really want, and she's sitting right across the room."

"Speak for yourself, brother," Liam said and then finished off his beer.

"Excuse me, gentlemen. Your...um...ladies wanted me to tell you that they left." This came from the waiter their women had been ogling.

"Did they seem okay to drive?" Will asked, showing concern.

"You must be Will," the waiter said.

"Yes."

"Okay, then. Megan said to tell you that she's perfectly fine and she'll meet you at her place later."

"Any message for me?" Finn asked.

"Which one are you?" the waiter said.

Poor guy. Their women had obviously used him to impart information on their way out. Connor smiled at the thought of it.

"I'm Finn, the best and the brightest O'Brien brother," he said.

Connor and Liam shook their heads, and Will let out a laugh.

"Let's see. Harper is yours, right?" the waiter said.

"Or so he likes to think," Connor teased. "It's really the other way around."

"Right. Well, Harper said to tell you she'll wait up for you."

"Oooohhhhh," Liam said. "Somebody's going to get lucky tonight."

"Yeah, and it's obviously not you!" Finn said.

Liam gave him the finger, which they all ignored. This was typical behavior for the brothers, and even Will seemed to be getting used to it.

"So, which one of you is Connor?" the waiter asked, looking between the two remaining brothers.

Liam raised his hand, and Connor smacked it down. "That would be me," Connor said firmly.

"Okay. Julia said to have fun and that she'll talk to you in the morning."

It might not have been as enticing a message as Finn and Will had gotten, but Connor smiled all the same. He could read between the lines, and he understood what Julia had been trying to tell him. She knew how much he'd needed a night out, and she was giving him free rein to stay as long as he wanted. Which meant that she was sensitive to his needs and that she trusted him. That was huge in his book, especially since Cam had come back into his life. The fact that Julia trusted him made his heart warm. Maybe love was the right word to describe this feeling after all.

"Now, let me think," the waiter said, tapping his index finger to his chin. "There was one other message."

All heads turned toward Liam, who wore an expression of surprise and hope.

"McKayla, the pretty blonde one."

"Yeah, that's right. What did she say?" Liam asked, not bothering to hide his impatience.

"She said, and I quote, 'Keep your nose out of my business.'"

Before Liam could react, Finn and Connor burst out laughing. Will was the only one who had the decency to look sorry.

"Are you serious, man?" Liam asked as if the waiter might have gotten him confused with someone else.

"You're Liam, right?"

"That's right."

"Well, then, yes. Sorry, man." And with that, the waiter turned and walked away. A few minutes later, Liam left, not even bothering with excuses.

"I gotta go," he mumbled, and that was it.

"Gosh, that sucks," Will said, shaking his head.

Connor snickered but not so much about Liam as about Will using the word "gosh." He was as straight as an arrow, that one.

"He'll get over it," Finn said and then finished off the last of his beer. "You guys about ready to go? I've got a pretty lady waiting at home for me."

"Me too," Will said.

"I guess that leaves me, huh?" Connor said, although being alone had never really bothered him. In fact, he usually enjoyed it, or he had until recently. But suddenly, the idea of sitting there drinking alone didn't appeal to him. He'd much rather be going home to Julia. *Damn! Maybe I really do love her.*

They'd made Will the designated driver, although they'd all driven there separately. It turned out that none of them had drunk enough to need Will's services, which was probably a good thing. But it also made Connor feel old. They were all starting to "settle down" even though none of them were married yet. He'd bet money that it wouldn't be long before Finn proposed to Harper. And now Connor had Ava and Julia. And if Liam had his way, he'd be tangled up with McKayla before long.

What a crazy thought. Just a matter of months ago, Connor had been as free as a bird, flitting between women and not even considering settling down. And now he was the father of a beautiful baby girl, who, if he were being honest, he missed like crazy whenever they were apart.

Suddenly, he didn't want to be free as a bird anymore. He wanted to be the involved dad— a man who was there for his daughter from now until forever. But when he looked into the future, it wasn't just Ava's face he saw. He saw Julia's face too.

Oh. My. God. I do love her!

"Hey, Connor? Something wrong?" Finn asked, breaking into his thoughts.

"No. But, I just decided that I'm ready to get out of here too." He might not have someone waiting at home, but he knew right where he wanted to be.

Up until then, it had been easy to forget that Will was Julia's cousin. First, they didn't look that much alike, and second, Will had just been one of the guys. But now Will studied him closely.

"I have to admit that at first, I wasn't so sure about Julia dating you. But now I can see how much she cares about you," Will said.

"Goes both ways," Connor said, looking him directly in the eyes.

"I can see that."

"I wish it were that easy for the rest of her family."

"You're talking about Dr. Lee, right?"

Connor shrugged.

"I get it. He's my uncle, but he's always scared the crap out of me," Will said. "I'm related to Julia through Debra."

Connor smiled at Will's attempt to apologize for Julia's dad.

"Anyway, he's just overprotective because Julia's his only child," Will said.

Connor could relate. He'd become fiercely protective of his own daughter in the short time he'd known her, and he suspected the feeling would continue to grow. While he and Will had been talking, Finn had paid their tab, and now he stood, indicating that guys' night was officially over.

Connor and Will stood too, all three of them anxious to get back to their women. They said goodbye in the parking lot and took off in their separate vehicles. As Connor drove through town and then down the two-lane road toward his house, he debated about turning around and heading to Julia's.

He felt confident that if he showed up on her doorstep, she'd let him in and even invite him to spend the night, but he decided that wasn't the best course of action. His thoughts were all over the place, and he needed some time to process what he'd discovered— that he loved her.

He was afraid that if he went to her house, they'd tumble into bed together, and then he'd tell her he loved her before, during, or after they had sex. And for some reason, he didn't want it to go down that way. He wanted to tell her in the light of day when she least expected it, not during the throes of passion. Maybe it was because of the way their relationship had begun. Originally, that's what he'd thought it had been about—sex. But now he knew different, and he wanted her to believe him when he said the words.

So, even though his body yearned for her and he would have liked nothing better than to be wrapped up in her arms, he went straight home. But as for going straight to sleep, that wasn't going to happen. Instead, he lay there in the dark, hands behind his head, and tried to formulate a plan for when he would tell her. After a half-hour of thinking, he realized he sucked at making plans. He was much better at shooting from the hip, at spontaneity. Julia was the one who excelled at planning, not him.

"Errrrrrr," he growled after several more minutes went by and he still hadn't come up with an idea. But then he decided to cut himself some slack. He would know when the time was right, and then he would go for it.

"Ahhh. Much better," he said, wriggling down beneath the sheet. After all, Julia knew him, and she wouldn't expect some big production. He would do what he did best—play it by ear and then hope like hell that she'd say it back.

Chapter 24

"I recently started giving her solid food," Cam said, "so if she seems hungry, you can try to feed her from one of the jars I brought." She proceeded to hold up jars of baby food ranging from fruit to mixed veggies to cereal.

"We'll be fine, won't we, sweetheart?" Julia said as she gave Ava a squeeze. This was the first time she'd seen Cam since Connor had had "the talk" with her. It had been awkward at first, but the minute Cam had handed Ava to her, Julia's discomfort had disappeared.

Oddly enough, Cam had agreed to let Julia watch Ava while Connor and his brothers helped Cam move into her new apartment. Julia took that as a positive sign, since Cam could have left Ava with her parents instead.

Connor winked at Julia. "I'm not sure who's going to have more fun, you or Ava."

Julia smiled broadly while Cam looked on. While she didn't want to rub Cam's nose in it, she had decided not to hide the way she felt about Connor or Ava. It was time that everyone started getting used to this, Cam included.

"I need to get some tie-downs from the garage. Be right back," Connor said.

After he left the room, Julia and Cam stared at each other for a moment, and Julia hefted Ava to her other hip. "She's getting heavier," Julia said, hoping to break the ice.

"I know. Ever since she started on solids, I can tell a difference," Cam said, reaching out to touch Ava's hand.

"Connor said your new apartment is really nice. I bet you're looking forward to moving in."

Cam nodded. "It will be great for Ava to have her own room. We've been sharing my old bedroom at my parents' house, and it's kind of crowded."

"I bet. It's amazing how much stuff babies need."

After a brief pause, they both started talking at once.

"I…"

"Look…"

"You go ahead," Julia said.

"I just wanted to say that I appreciate you helping out with Ava."

"It's my pleasure."

"And I'm…sorry. For the way I treated you before."

Julia tried not to let her mouth fall open, but Cam obviously read her look of shock.

"This has been really tough on me, and I guess I was hoping…well, I thought…"

"That you, Connor, and Ava would become a family," Julia finished for her.

Cam nodded. "But now that I know that's not going to happen, I need to move on."

"Just to clarify, that doesn't mean moving *away*, right?"

"I considered moving back to Denver, but I don't think that would be best for Ava."

Thank God.

"Besides Connor, she has a lot of other people here who love her."

Julia nodded. "Myself included."

Just then, Connor swept back into the room, loaded down with various straps. He looked between the two women, and not noticing any signs of discord, he smiled. "We should get going," he said to Cam.

Cam started to follow him, but then she turned back around and said to Julia, "I should give you my phone number, just in case."

"She can just call me," Connor said, but then he clamped his mouth shut when Julia frowned at him. "Never mind. Julia should have your number too. I'll just wait outside." With that, he took turns kissing Julia and Ava on the cheek and then sauntered out the door.

"Men can be so oblivious sometimes," Cam said, her mouth turning up into a semblance of a smile.

Julia laughed. "Yet they think they know everything."

"Exactly."

Julia set Ava down in the middle of the carpet while she and Cam exchanged phone numbers. Then Cam bent down to give Ava a squeeze.

At least she's not wearing a V-neck today.

When she stood back up, Cam said, "I'm not completely over feeling jealous of you and Connor."

It sounded like a warning, but her expression didn't contain the malice that it had before.

"Same here," Julia said, surprising herself with her bluntness.

Her admission seemed to take Cam aback too. "Really? You're jealous of me?"

"You were the first woman he loved, and you gave him a child. I'd say that gives me two valid reasons to be jealous."

Cam shook her head. "But he loves you now. Surely, you know that."

Julia's eyes widened, but she didn't have time to respond.

"Uh, Cam? You about ready to go?" Connor said through the screen door.

Julia felt a moment of panic, wondering if he'd heard what Cam had just said, but he appeared to be his usual easygoing self.

"Coming. I was just giving Julia some last-minute instructions."

"Okay," he said and retreated again.

"See what I mean? He doesn't have a clue about what we were really talking about."

Julia giggled, but it came out strained.

"Call me if something comes up with Ava," Cam called over her shoulder before disappearing out the door.

After they left, Julia slumped down on the rug next to Ava and handed her a toy. Ava babbled enthusiastically and temporarily distracted Julia from her rambling thoughts.

Is it true? Does Connor love me? Did he tell Cam that? No. He wouldn't tell her before he told me. Would he?

She'd probably been sitting there with Ava for all of twenty minutes before the doorbell rang.

"Hello," Harper called through the screen.

"Come on in," Julia said, not wanting to get up and leave Ava alone.

But it wasn't just Harper who'd come to visit. McKayla entered the room too, and each of them was carrying a bag from a local children's clothing store.

"We come bearing gifts," Harper sang as she and McKayla plopped down on the floor next to Julia and Ava.

"Ohmigod. She's the cutest thing ever!" McKayla exclaimed.

"I told you," Harper said.

"Well, you're her aunt, so I would expect you to say that," McKayla said.

Harper stared at her like she'd said something crazy. "I'm not her aunt."

"Yet," McKayla said. "But you will be soon."

"Do you know something I don't?"

McKayla shook her head and reached out to hold Ava's hand.

Julia looked between the sisters with a touch of envy. How she'd wished she had a sibling, and now she was surrounded by people who had them. Connor, Finn, and Liam, Harper and McKayla. While it would have been nice to have someone be related to her by blood, this was the next best thing.

"What's in the bags?" Julia asked.

"Here. See for yourself," Harper said, handing her a bag.

"Shouldn't Cam be the one to open these?"

Harper shook her head. "We didn't buy them for Cam. We bought them for Ava, and we wanted to give them to her when you were here."

Tears pricked the corner of her eyes at her friends' show of support. Julia leaned over to give

Harper a hug, and then she hugged McKayla too for good measure.

"Geez, you two are sappy. Just open it!" McKayla said.

Julia reached into Harper's bag first and pulled out an adorable two-piece outfit. The shirt read *If you think I'm cute, you should see my daddy!* The set also came with a matching bib.

"How sweet! Connor will love it!" Julia said.

"Now mine," McKayla said.

McKayla's gift was a colorful floral-print sundress and matching sunhat.

"Wow. This little girl is going to be so spoiled," Julia said just as the doorbell rang again.

"Hellllloooo," Barbara called through the screen before letting herself in.

Julia had known that Harper might stop by, but she'd had no idea that Mrs. O'Brien was coming over. Not that she should have been surprised. Everyone knew how thrilled Barbara was to finally have a grandchild. It was all Connor could do to prevent her from coming over every time Ava was there, claiming he still needed to bond with her on his own.

But Barbara wasn't one to sit back and wait for an invitation.

"Hello, girls," she said as she bustled into the room. She didn't wait for a reply as she bent over and lifted Ava into her arms. "There's my sweet baby," she said, hugging Ava to her chest.

Ava must have sensed that this woman was going to be important to her since she flapped her arms happily and gave her grandmother a wide toothless grin.

"Isn't she just the most precious baby you've ever seen?" Barbara said without looking at anyone but her granddaughter.

Julia felt a twinge of jealousy, knowing that Cam had helped to create this "most precious baby," but she quickly let it go. No matter who had birthed Ava, Barbara would have said the same thing.

"Barbara, have you met my sister, McKayla?" Harper said, changing the subject.

"No, I haven't, but I heard that you work for my boys. It's very nice to meet you," Barbara said as she plunked down on the couch with Ava still in her arms.

So much for spending quality time with Ava this evening, Julia thought as she looked around the room. But she couldn't blame them for wanting to get to know the newest addition to the family. Even though, technically, only Barbara and Ava were family.

"Now, Harper, when are you and Finn going to get married and give me some more grandchildren?" Barbara said with a twinkle in her bright blue eyes.

Barbara was in her sixties, but she still had a vibrant energy about her. Her short, stylish hair was dark brown with auburn highlights, and every time Julia had seen her, she'd been fashionably dressed. She had a warm, confident air about her that drew people in even though her bluntness could be shocking at times.

"Um…" Harper stuttered.

"Maybe you should be asking Finn that question," McKayla said without flinching.

Now, there was an interesting match!

Harper scowled at her sister, but McKayla didn't pay any attention.

Barbara laughed heartily, and Ava gave a little laugh too.

Then, looking directly at Julia, Barbara said, "And what about you and Connor?"

"Me?" Julia said, realizing too late that she was the only one Barbara could be referring to.

"Yes. This little girl could use a sister or brother."

Julia racked her brain for a response but came up empty.

"Oh boy. I think Ava just made a poo-poo," Barbara said, wrinkling up her nose.

They all laughed, and Julia was relieved that she'd been saved by Ava's "poo-poo!"

"Where's the diaper bag?" Barbara asked while holding Ava away from her chest.

"How about if we take care of it?" Harper suggested. "McKayla, why don't you stay here and keep Mrs. O'Brien company for a few minutes?"

Harper didn't wait for a response. She simply took Ava from Barbara and motioned to Julia, who grabbed the diaper bag and followed her down the hall to the spare bedroom.

Once they were safely behind the closed door, Julia let out a loud sigh. "Thank you," she said.

Harper had laid Ava down and was rummaging through the diaper bag. "Barbara really knows how to put someone on the spot, huh?"

But Harper didn't seem to be as thrown by it as Julia was. Of course, she'd known the O'Briens a lot longer than Julia had and was probably used to Barbara's personality.

"How do you feel about having her for a mother-in-law?" Julia asked as she handed Harper a wet wipe.

Harper plugged her nose with one hand while she used the wipe with the other.

"Well…" she said, sounding funny because her nose was plugged.

Julia giggled. "Here. Let me finish," she said, nudging Harper aside. She'd had plenty of practice with this from working at her dad's office, and she finished changing the diaper with crisp efficiency.

Wrapping the soiled diaper in a tight ball, she tucked it inside a plastic bag, which she tied and handed to Harper.

"Oh, great. So, I'm stuck holding the sh—"

"Shhh," Julia warned. "Don't say that word in front of Ava."

Harper giggled. "Right, because she's smart enough to understand it already!"

Julia picked up Ava and gave her a hug. "There you go. All clean."

"You're a pro at this, Jules."

"I love babies. You know that."

"I know, but it's really special how you've taken to Ava when she's…"

"Not even mine. I know. It's strange, but I'm trying not to think of it like that anymore. She's part of Connor, and I love…oops!"

Harper's eyes danced. "You love him! I knew it!"

"Shhhhh," Julia implored.

"Why? Ava won't mind if you love her daddy, will you, sweetie?" Harper said as she tugged on Ava's bare toes.

"Don't say a word about this, Harper. I mean it. I haven't even told him yet."

"I won't. I promise," Harper said solemnly.

"Right. Like you promised not to tell him when I went up to the lake house?"

"That was Connor's fault. He pressured me into it. This is different."

"You're right, and I want to be the first one to tell him."

"When?"

Julia shrugged. "I'm not sure yet. There's a lot going on right now."

"No time like the present," Harper said.

"I seem to recall you holding out on Finn for quite some time," Julia reminded her.

"Yes, but I've made up for it since then," she said, wiggling her eyebrows.

Julia laughed. "We better get back out there before Barbara gets suspicious."

"Ha. She'd probably be happy if she knew we were talking about loving her sons. That just means more grandchildren for her."

"Maybe from you and Finn, but Connor and I still have a long way to go."

Harper shook her head. "I don't think so, Jules. He already has one child. What's a few more?"

Julia rolled her eyes, but she was secretly thrilled at the idea. She'd always wanted a big family, and if she were to become part of the O'Brien clan, she'd already be starting out with a large group of people. It was a heady thought, and she practically floated back out to the living room with Ava tucked securely against her hip.

"It must have been a really bad one for it to have taken that long!" Barbara exclaimed.

McKayla was perched on the edge of the chair across from Barbara, looking shell-shocked, and Julia wondered what had transpired between them while she and Harper had been occupied.

Surprisingly, when Harper stood up to leave a short while later, Barbara rose too.

"Sorry for hogging her," Barbara said as she handed Ava back to Julia. "I just can't get enough of this little cutie."

"I understand," Julia said, following Barbara, Harper, and McKayla to the door.

After exchanging goodbyes and thanking her friends for the gifts, Julia shut the door behind them and returned to the living room. Ava looked sleepy from all the activity, so Julia sat in Connor's newly acquired rocking chair by the window and gently rocked her to sleep.

Julia must have been tired too because, the next thing she knew, she was being awakened by a kiss on her cheek. Thinking it might have been a dream, she slowly blinked open her eyes to find Connor staring down at her with the sweetest expression she'd ever seen plastered all over his handsome face.

Chapter 25

"Hi," Julia said.

"Hi."

"I must have fallen asleep while I was rocking her."

"Did she wear you out?"

Julia glanced down at the sleeping bundle in her arms. "No, but I think my arm might have fallen asleep from staying in this position for so long."

Connor laughed. "Here. Let me take her."

"Careful," Julia said as she gently transferred Ava into his outstretched arms.

Ava stirred, but she didn't wake up.

"What time is it? Where's Cam?"

"It's nine o'clock. I convinced Cam to let Ava stay here tonight."

"Really? Where's she going to sleep?"

"Cam sent me home with a portable crib. I thought I'd set it up in my bedroom for tonight, but I'll eventually have to get something more permanent."

Julia nodded. "That's a good sign, right? Cam letting you keep Ava overnight."

"It took some convincing, but yeah. She was exhausted after the move, and I offered to keep Ava so she could get a good night's sleep."

"That was sweet of you."

"It has nothing to do with being sweet. I want Ava with me as much as possible, Jules."

"I know," she said, admiring the way he looked with Ava cradled in his muscular arms.

"Maybe I should set up the crib so I can lay her down. She's starting to get heavy."

Julia giggled. "Now is the only time she'd be okay with you saying that. Babies are supposed to be chunky. Do you want me to hold her while you set up the crib?"

"Sure."

They made the transfer again, and this time, Ava whimpered. She popped her eyes open and looked right at Julia, but then her eyelids grew heavy, and she fell back asleep.

Connor took the fold-up crib that he'd leaned against the front door and started walking down the hall toward his bedroom. "You coming?" he asked over his shoulder.

"Yeah."

She stood in the doorway and watched while he set up the portable crib in an open corner of his room.

"You do realize that you'd still be able to hear her if she was in the spare room, right?" Julia teased.

"Maybe, but I'm a pretty deep sleeper. What if she needed something and I didn't hear her right away?"

Julia thought it was sweet that he was being so protective, so she didn't protest. Once he finished with the crib, he said, "Should we change her first?"

Julia shook her head. "She had a huge blowout not long ago, so I think she'll be good for a while." She carefully set Ava in the crib and covered her with the blanket that Cam had provided.

"Excuse me. Did you just say *blowout?*"

The look on his face was priceless, and if Ava hadn't been sleeping, Julia would have rolled with laughter. Instead, she just smiled and said, "You don't want to know."

Connor sat down on the edge of his bed and raked his hand through his cropped hair. As she came and sat beside him, she realized that he looked tired too. Leaning her head on his shoulder, she said, "It's been a long day. I should leave and let you get some sleep."

"What? No. I mean stay...please."

Looking up at him through her lashes, she melted. "Do you want me to stay and help with Ava?"

"No. I mean...yes and no. I really want you to stay for me."

"Oh."

Sitting together in the dark with the sound of Ava's steady breathing as background noise, the scene felt oddly intimate. It was something she'd expect to do with her own child someday—sit there and watch him or her with wonder. It felt very...cozy.

"Lie down with me," Connor said.

"Are you sure? What if we wake her up?"

But Connor was already pulling back the covers, and then he started undressing.

After he'd removed his shirt, he unzipped his pants and stepped out of them, leaving on his underwear.

At any other time, the display of flesh would have tempted Julia, but now she looked over at Ava's sleeping form and felt uncertain.

"We don't have to do anything, Jules. Just let me hold you."

She looked at him strangely, and he said, "I know. There's a first time for everything."

Smiling, she walked around to the opposite side of the bed and started removing her clothes. Connor lay on his side, his head propped in one hand, and watched as if he'd never seen her before. When she was down to her bra and panties, she crawled up next to him and felt his arms come around her.

"How's that?" he whispered against her hair.

"Perfect." And it was. She was lying beside the man she loved with a baby asleep in the crib across from them.

Rubbing her palm over his chest, she began to talk, telling him all about the visit with his mom, Harper, and McKayla.

"I knew my mom would find a way to sneak over here," he said, amused.

"Who can blame her? It's her first grandchild."

Connor was tracing patterns on her back, and she felt her body warming with every stroke. It was impossible to lie in bed with him and not want him to touch her like this. She'd be shocked if they made it through the night without making love.

"I'm sure there will be more," he said quietly.

"True. Harper and Finn will probably get married soon, and I know they want kids."

Brushing her hair back with his fingertips, he said, "I'm not talking about Harper and Finn."

"Oh." Julia's heart skipped a beat, but she was afraid to think he was talking about them.

"Well, it doesn't seem very likely for Liam since he's not dating anyone right now…"

"Julia?"

"Um-hmm?" Her heart was racing, and she willed herself to calm down.

"I'm not talking about Liam either."

"Then that leaves…"

"Us."

Her eyes flicked upward to connect with his, and what she saw there took her breath away. He gazed down at her with such intensity, such emotion, that she was temporarily rendered speechless. With one hand resting on her hip, he cupped her chin with the other as if to keep her locked in place.

"I didn't want to do it like this," he said, his voice catching.

"Do what?"

"Julia?"

"Yes?"

And then Ava shifted in her crib and let out a little cry.

They both stilled, waiting to see if she'd go back to sleep. But then came another cry and some rustling noises.

Connor sighed as Julia moved out of his arms.

"Maybe she's just cold," Julia said. She padded across the room and leaned over the crib. Sure enough, Ava had kicked off her blanket, but her eyes were wide open, and when she saw Julia, she broke into a sweet smile.

Julia hadn't noticed that Connor had gotten up too until she felt his warm body up against her back and his arms snaked around her waist. Resting his head on her shoulder, he peered down at Ava.

"Looks like she's up," he said with a touch of regret in his voice.

"We'll have to get used to this—being interrupted I mean. How about if you pick her up while I go warm up a bottle?"

"Sure," he said.

Glancing around for the nearest clothing item, she picked up his T-shirt from the floor and pulled it over her head before going out to the kitchen. As she was coming back down the hall toward his bedroom, she stopped in her tracks. *Is he singing?* She stood and listened for a few seconds, smiling to herself as she hit the crescendo. And then she slipped back into the room.

Connor was sitting up against the headboard with Ava perched on his thighs. His large hands engulfed her little back, and she appeared to be enraptured by his version of Bon Jovi's "Livin' on a Prayer."

Suddenly, he glanced up and noticed Julia standing there, and she swore she saw his face flush.

"Bon Jovi? Out of all the songs in the entire world, that was the song you chose?" she teased as she climbed onto the bed and sat next to him.

"I couldn't think of anything else."

"Didn't your mom ever sing you nursery rhymes?"

"I'm sure she did, but I couldn't remember any of them. Besides, I was under pressure."

Julia giggled and handed him the bottle. "Here. As much as she seemed to enjoy your singing, I think she wants this more."

Taking the bottle from her, he adjusted Ava's position so she was cradled against his chest, and he put the bottle to her lips. The scene was so natural, so beautiful, that Julia got a lump in her throat. Suddenly, everything meshed together in her mind. Maybe she and Connor had come together for this very reason, to not only love each other but to love this little girl too.

Neither of them spoke as they watched Ava contentedly suck down her formula, her eyes beginning to droop once again.

"I still can't believe she's mine," Connor said softly.

Julia squeezed his arm. "I know. She's so beautiful, Connor."

"So are you," he said, turning his head toward her.

Leaning in, she gave him a quick kiss on the lips in lieu of a thank you. When she pulled away, she noticed that the bottle had slipped out of Ava's mouth and formula was dribbling down her chin.

"Here," she said, handing Connor the burp cloth she'd brought in with the bottle.

He took it from her, threw it over his broad shoulder, and immediately hoisted Ava up. Patting her back with just the right amount of pressure, she emitted a burp and then nestled her face into the crook of his neck.

Julia couldn't help but think what a stunning picture they made—daddy and daughter together. If Harper were there, she would have snapped a thousand photos by now. Then again, Julia wouldn't want Harper to be there with Connor looking all rumpled and sexy in his underwear.

He looked completely at ease with Ava resting on his shoulder, and once again, Julia was amazed at how much had changed in such a short time. When she'd first met Connor, she would have never pictured him like this—sexy *and* sweet. She'd been so caught up in the sexy…

Suddenly, he shifted beside her and carefully climbed off the bed. She admired his backside as he walked softly to the crib and gently laid Ava back down before pulling the blanket up over her. When he turned back around, he caught Julia staring, and his face broke out into a sexy grin.

Crawling back into bed, he pulled her close and said, "Now. Where were we?"

"I think you were about to make love to me."

"I thought we were talking," he said, although his eyes widened to mammoth proportions when she whipped off his T-shirt and tossed it onto the floor.

"We'll talk later," she said as she reached around and unhooked her bra. He swallowed hard when she slid down the straps to reveal her bare breasts, which were heaving with desire. Leaving her underwear on for now, she crawled over his lap and settled herself on his hips before wrapping her arms around his neck.

"I thought you were worried about waking Ava," he said as his hands came up to cup her breasts.

"We'll just have to be quiet," she said, thrusting her chest forward to fill his generous hands.

"It was my singing, wasn't it? That's what got you all riled up," he teased, flicking his thumbs across her taut nipples.

She smiled and shook her head, undulating her hips against his. "Guess again."

He groaned as his erection rubbed up against her core. "Can't…really…think straight." And then he dipped his head to her chest and drew a nipple deep into his warm mouth.

Massaging her fingers into his scalp, she held his head in place as he sucked and nipped at her breasts. Her legs tightened on either side of his as she rubbed along his erection.

Dropping his hands from her breasts, he reached around to cup her backside and lifted her off him. Expecting him to get a condom, she was surprised when he said, "Stay just like that."

And then he dipped his hand down the front of her panties and cupped her sex.

"Connor," she said on a deep exhale.

"Shhh. Quiet."

Nodding, she placed one hand over her mouth and braced herself against him with the other. After teasing her damp folds, he inserted a finger deep inside, causing her to tighten her core around him. He played with her, alternating between soft strokes and deep penetration, until she was bucking into his hand, her head tipped back, one hand still clamped over her mouth.

"You feel so good," he whispered against her belly, his warm breath fluttering against her damp skin.

Why was it that whenever one was supposed to be quiet, there was an overwhelming urge to cry out? She did her best to stifle her moans in her hand as Connor urged her on.

"I can feel you getting close," he said and then nipped the underside of her breast.

And that was all it took. Gripping his shoulder tightly, she saw a burst of light behind her eyes, and she came repeatedly, all while trying to remain quiet. Just when she thought her knees might give out, he gently rolled her onto her back and slipped off her panties while she attempted to catch her breath.

Still in a daze, she heard him open the drawer of his nightstand, remove his underwear, and then rip open a condom packet before coming back over her. Supporting his weight on one strong forearm, he took hold of his erection and slowly immersed himself, her legs opening wide to accommodate him. Winding her arms around his neck, she pulled him down and kissed him deeply.

Moaning against her mouth, he lowered one hand to grip her hip as he thrust into her. Even though she'd just climaxed, she was still aroused, and as the friction built between them, she felt on the verge of another orgasm.

Abandoning her mouth, he buried his head in her neck, where he nipped the sensitive skin and then licked it, sending a spark of desire straight to her core.

Running her hands over his back, she reveled in the feel of his muscles contracting as he pounded into her while trying to remain as quiet as possible.

When she cupped his buttocks to pull him in even further, they both lost it—first him and then her. Afterward, they stayed connected until their breathing came down, and then Connor kissed her on the tip of her nose and whispered, "Be right back."

While he was in the bathroom, Julia found his T-shirt, slipped it back on, and padded over to the crib to check on Ava. She was still sleeping soundly, her thumb partway in her mouth and one arm flung out to the side.

Julia tiptoed back to the bed and slid beneath the covers. It was then that she realized they'd never finished their conversation from earlier, the one about Barbara wanting more grandkids. How she'd love to give Ava a half-brother, half-sister, or both someday.

But is that what Connor had been alluding to? She shook her head. Maybe he'd been joking around or speaking hypothetically.

She convinced herself that she'd misunderstood, because why would he be talking about having more kids when they hadn't even exchanged I love yous yet?

Chapter 26

The next few weeks were a whirlwind of activity. The summer season had finally descended on Michigan, and Connor and his brothers were busy from sunup until sundown with hardly a moment's rest. Their client list had expanded since they'd opened a storefront in downtown Brandon, and they were gaining more clients every day.

In the meantime, Connor and Cam had agreed that Ava would stay with him three nights a week, plus every other weekend. While he would have liked it to be more, he felt like the arrangement was fair.

He looked forward to his time with Ava more than he'd ever thought possible, and he always felt a letdown when Cam came to pick her up. But on the bright side, he and Cam were cooperating, and for that he was grateful.

Julia had been a huge help too, first, by transforming the spare room into a nursery for Ava, and second, by staying over on the nights that Ava was there. She'd taken great pleasure in choosing the theme for the nursery, and he'd let her decorate it to her heart's content. If it had been left up to him, he'd have bought a crib and a dresser and called it good.

But now, when he went into Ava's room, it was like stepping into a Walt Disney film. There were princesses everywhere: on the wallpaper border, the crib bedding, and even the lamp. Julia had been trying unsuccessfully to teach him the names of all the Disney princesses, insisting that this information would somehow be useful to him. Now, in addition to his action movies, he had a collection of Disney DVDs. He was beginning to wonder if this obsession had less to do with Ava and more to do with Julia. But Julia seemed happy, and that was all that mattered.

He wasn't sure if it was good or bad that he'd started humming Disney tunes when he was at work, but according to Liam, it was the latter.

"Dude? What are you singing?" Liam had said one day.

Connor hadn't realized that he was singing the theme song from *Frozen*, until Liam had stared at him with a look of irritation and amusement.

"Get your head out of your ass. Even I know that song!" Finn had said.

Luckily, that had brought an end to the conversation, but after that, Connor had tried not to sing Disney songs in front of his brothers.

He'd also noticed that his house had been inundated with the color pink. It was everywhere—on blankets, toys, and clothes—but he couldn't blame it all on Julia. His mom, Harper, McKayla, and Cam were also at fault. The closet in Ava's room was already full, and she was under one year old! Not to mention the dresser drawers that were bulging with clothes, many of which still had tags on them. His little girl couldn't even walk, yet she owned more clothes than he did.

"Babies outgrow things quickly," Julia had said when he'd questioned her about it. "Plus, they stain things, so they need a lot of changes of clothes."

Knowing his mom and the other women in his life would probably agree, he'd let the matter drop. Besides, Ava always looked adorable thanks to these same women.

Julia wasn't the only one who had jumped in to help. Barbara had offered to babysit Ava a few days a week while Cam was at work. At first, he hadn't been sure Cam would go for it, but she didn't have a lot of other options, so she'd agreed to it on a trial basis. But when Barbara agreed to babysit Ava at Cam's apartment, it had erased any reservations she'd had. And if for some reason Barbara wasn't available, his other family members would pitch in in a heartbeat.

Yes, his little princess now had everyone he knew wrapped around her little finger. The only people she hadn't met yet were Julia's parents, but that would change soon. Julia had arranged for her parents to come over to his house next Sunday so they could finally meet Ava. While he was still skeptical about Dr. Lee's opinion of him, Julia had assured him that once they met Ava, that would all change. He had no choice but to take her word for it.

Words. Between work and spending time with Ava, he'd been so busy that he hadn't found the right time to tell Julia how he felt. That he loved her.

He thought about it often enough, and it had been right on the tip of his tongue several times, but they'd either been interrupted or he'd chickened out. He hated to admit that he was scared, even to himself. While he considered himself assertive and confident in most things, he felt like a novice when it came to love.

Looking back, he realized that what he'd had with Cam had been more of an infatuation than love. With Cam, he hadn't looked beyond a particular day or week, but with Julia, he was thinking long term. He could easily imagine being married to her, having kids with her, and meshing their lives together. She already fit in with his family, and everybody loved her. If he were being honest, they probably liked her more than they liked him sometimes. And who could blame them?

Julia was perfect for him, and they were good together. He wanted to build a life with her, and he hoped she wanted the same thing too. Now, if he could only man up and tell her that.

Chapter 27

On one of Connor's weekends with Ava, Julia suggested they take her to Independence Oaks, a local park that offered walking trails, picnic areas, and a swimming pond. So, after packing and re-packing the diaper bag to account for all possibilities, and loading a cooler with sandwiches, fruit, and drinks, they were off.

It was one of those glorious days in June that felt like summer even though it wasn't technically summer yet. Julia had dressed Ava in a lightweight cotton outfit (pink, of course) that covered her skin, plus a matching sunhat.

"It's eighty degrees. Is all that stuff really necessary?" Connor asked.

"Do you want your daughter to burn?" Julia replied.

"No."

"Well, then, yes. All of this stuff is necessary."

Julia had become just as protective as he was especially when Ava was on their watch. The last thing she wanted was for something bad to happen and for Cam to blame it on her. They'd formed a tentative bond over these past several weeks, and she didn't want anything to jeopardize it. Instead of looking at

Cam as the enemy or as someone to be jealous of, Julia had started thinking of her as a part of a team—team Ava.

And for the most part, it seemed to be working. There were still occasions where Julia would catch Cam staring at her and Connor with something akin to envy, but for the most part, she'd been respectful. One evening, when Connor had been working late, Julia had been the one at his house when Cam brought Ava over. After Cam had imparted information about Ava's eating and sleeping schedule, Julia had taken the opportunity to make small talk with her. She hadn't done it to become Cam's best friend but to make things more comfortable between them. Ultimately, she'd done it for Connor and Ava.

"How's it going at work?" Julia asked as she set Ava's bottles in the refrigerator.

Cam appeared surprised by the show of interest, but she quickly recovered. "Not bad. I feel better about being there now that Barb is watching Ava."

Barb? Interesting. Everyone else called Connor's mom Barbara. Cam must have been feeling more comfortable with her too.

"Having her babysit is a lot better than having to use daycare," Julia said.

Cam nodded. She had sat down at the kitchen table and was still holding Ava in her lap as if she were reluctant to leave her. For all the negative feelings Julia had had at the beginning, she'd realized that Cam was a good mom and was trying to do her best for her daughter.

Sitting down at the table across from her, Julia said, "Would you like something to drink?"

"Oh. No thanks. I'm actually meeting someone for drinks in just a little while."

Do I dare ask? "Oh. A friend?"

"A co-worker," Cam replied.

Julia thought that might be the end of the discussion, but Cam continued talking as if she'd wanted to say more all along.

"A man, actually. His name's Tony."

Julia wasn't surprised. Cam was an intelligent, beautiful woman, and it was easier to admit that now that she'd stopped pursuing Connor.

"He asked me out a few weeks ago, but I said no. I didn't think it was a good idea since we work together and because of Ava. But he asked again, and I caved."

Julia laughed because it seemed like a common theme for the women in her life—herself included. "That good looking, huh?"

Smiling her perfect Barbie-doll smile, Cam said, "Yeah."

"That'll do it every time."

"Is that what happened for you with Connor?"

Uh-oh. Now they were stepping into dangerous territory.

"Sorry. That's really none of my business," Cam said, averting her eyes to Ava, who was happily banging a toy against the table.

"Do you really want to know?" Julia ventured.

"Only if you want to tell me."

Julia took a few seconds and then decided that this is what women do. They share. And since Cam was a woman and was sitting across the table, trying to be nice, she would share—to a point.

"As you probably know, the O'Brien brothers take care of all the lawn maintenance at Harper's house and studio where I work."

Cam nodded.

"Well, at first, I avoided Connor like the plague. I thought he was too smooth, too cocky."

"No argument here."

Trying not to think about Cam's firsthand knowledge of the man, Julia continued. "But he just never gave up. He kept asking me out until he caught me at a weak moment, and I finally said yes."

Cam giggled. "He can be very persistent."

"And like you with Tony, I couldn't deny my attraction to him."

"But at least you and Connor don't work together. I've been through this before, and it was a mistake."

"Are you talking about Tyler?"

Cam's smile evaporated. "Yes."

Julia didn't bother pointing out that Tyler was her boss *and* he was married—the double whammy. She assumed Cam had learned her lesson from that poor decision a long time ago.

"At least Tony is single," Cam said with a nervous laugh. And then, glancing down at her Kate Spade watch, she said, "I better get going."

With that, she stood up, kissed Ava on both cheeks, and then handed her to Julia.

When Cam had shown up in her formfitting floral print dress and high heels, Julia had assumed that she'd just come from work, but now she knew different. Cam had dressed to impress her date, just like most women would. Of course, not every woman looked like a model, but Julia could still relate.

Following her to the front door, Julia said, "I hope you and Tony have fun tonight."

"Thanks," Cam said, and then waving goodbye to Ava, she disappeared down the walkway.

After Cam had left, Julia felt pleased with herself. She'd planted the seeds of trust with Cam, and she couldn't wait to share the news with Connor when he came home. Oddly enough, she'd skimmed over some of what she and Cam had talked about, deciding that some things were better left unsaid.

Now, as they were walking around the lakeside trail at the park with Ava tucked into a baby carrier on Connor's chest, Julia wondered why he was so quiet.

"Everything okay?" she asked. He'd seemed distracted recently, and she'd assumed it was because of how busy he was. He'd been trying to balance work and parenthood as well as spending time with her, and she knew that he was exhausted.

She'd been offering her support in any way she could, including waking up with Ava in the middle of the night and letting him sleep in whenever possible, but he still seemed off.

"Yeah. Everything's fine. Why wouldn't it be?" Connor replied.

"Just wondered. I know how hard you've been working lately and…"

"It's not that."

"Okay."

"Sorry. I didn't mean to snap. I just have a lot on my mind."

Julia wasn't sure what else to say or how to make it better for him. "Do you want to take a break for a few minutes?"

They were about halfway around the trail, and she'd spotted a picnic table up ahead right by the water's edge.

"Yeah. That'll be good," he said.

Between the heat and carrying Ava, she figured he must be sweating. At least there was a breeze coming off the water, and she sat down beside him, facing the lake.

Pulling a teething ring out of the pocket of his cargo shorts, Connor handed it to Ava, who immediately plunked it into her mouth.

Then, inhaling deeply, he angled his body to face Julia, and his eyes locked onto hers. There was that intensity she'd been noticing lately, almost like he wanted to tell her something but didn't know how.

"What is it?' she said softly.

"I...I...shit!"

Eyes wide, she tried not to laugh. "Connor?"

"Sorry. I suck at this."

"This what?" Placing her hand on his forearm, she gave it a squeeze. "Just tell me." If things hadn't been going so well between them lately, she might have been nervous. But as it was, she just wanted him to be open with her. Their relationship had changed over the past several weeks, and she felt them getting closer and closer. She didn't want him to clam up on her now.

"Please," she added.

And then Ava dropped her teething ring on the ground, right in a patch of dirt at their feet.

"Don't swear!" Julia said when she saw Connor's mouth open. "I'll take care of it." Removing the small backpack she'd worn, she pulled out a pack of wet wipes and thoroughly cleaned off the toy before handing it back to Ava.

"You were saying?" Julia said without missing a beat.

Shaking his head and smiling, he said, "You're incredible. You know that?"

"All I did was clean it off," Julia replied, confused.

"No. It's not that. It's everything. You're just…incredible."

Is that what he's been trying to tell me for the past few weeks?

"Thank you?"

Connor tipped his head back and laughed, the rich sound filling the space around them. Then, taking one of her hands in one of his, he said, "You don't even know it, do you? How wonderful you are?"

From the way he was gazing at her, his eyes sparkling, his face lit up with a broad smile, she was finally starting to understand how much he appreciated her and maybe how much…

"I love you, Julia."

Whoa! Good thing they were sitting down, because she suddenly felt dizzy, and she gripped the edge of the picnic table for support.

"I've been trying to tell you for weeks, but I couldn't get it out. But I do. I love you." And then, before she had a chance to reply, he leaned forward and gently kissed her lips.

Ava chose that exact moment to show off her vocal abilities. "Wawawawawawa," she said, flapping her hands up and down excitedly.

Connor and Julia pulled apart to look in the same direction she was, and there, floating leisurely on the lake, were a pair of ducks, a mallard and his mate, not far from shore.

"Wawawawawa," Ava repeated.

"Maybe she's trying to say water," Julia said.

"She is pretty smart," Connor said proudly.

They watched the ducks for a minute before they swam away, and then Julia plunged the teething ring back in Ava's mouth.

"See. This is exactly what's been happening lately. You don't know how many times I started to tell you I love you and we've been interrupted."

Julia smiled, her heart bursting at the seams. "But Ava's the sweetest interruption ever."

Leaning down, he kissed her again, with a bit more zeal this time.

"We're in public," she reminded him after they pulled apart.

"Don't care."

"Connor?"

"Yeah," he mumbled against her lips.

"I love you too. You and Ava both."

"Thank God," he said, exhaling loudly.

Julia giggled, and then wrapping her arms around him and Ava, she gave them a big squeeze. After letting go, she said, "We should probably head back to the car and get the cooler. It's almost time for Ava's lunch."

"Not to mention yours," he teased.

"You know how I love my food."

"I hope not quite as much as you love me."

"I could never love anything that much. Well, except for this little girl," she said, tugging on Ava's toes.

As they trudged back up the hill to the trail, Connor said, "What about our own kids? Didn't you say you wanted two or three?"

If the sun hadn't been beating down on the top of her head, she might have thought she was dreaming. Were they really having this conversation? Was this really going to happen for them?

"You have a good memory," she said as their hands automatically entwined.

"I remember everything you've ever said to me."

"Even when I said you were cocky and too good looking?"

He chuckled. "Yes, even that. I hope I've proved you wrong."

Eyeing him up and down, she said, "Well, you're still good looking."

Squeezing her hand, he said, "I would love it if you still told me that twenty years from now."

"I guarantee it," she said, smiling up at him.

When they reached the Jeep, Connor took out the cooler while Julia changed Ava's diaper. Then they found a patch of grass underneath a sprawling maple tree and spread out a blanket.

"Ahhh. This is the life!" Connor said after they'd eaten. He had lain back with his hands behind his head, and Julia and Ava sat beside him.

Ava had just finished her bottle, and her little eyes were starting to close, her body going limp in Julia's arms. Julia felt like she could stay like this forever, just her, Connor, and Ava, their own little family.

"I love watching you with her," Connor said, breaking into her thoughts.

Julia smiled down at him. "I didn't even know you were looking."

"I can't wait to see you with our children someday."

Shifting her body to face him, she said, "When that happens, I'll still love Ava just as much. She may not share my blood, but she shares my heart, and she always will."

Sitting upright, Connor scooted next to her, wrapped an arm around her waist, and kissed her cheek.

"I know that," he said. "You're the most loving person I've ever known."

"You and Ava are easy to love," she said, her eyes misting over.

"I can't promise you that life will be perfect. But I can promise that I'll love you, and Ava, and our own children with everything I have. Forever."

And of that, she had no doubt.

Epilogue – Two Months Later

"We made it!" Julia said as they pulled up in front of the lake house.

"Barely!" Connor replied sarcastically, although he was smiling.

"We only had to stop a few times."

"I would say five times is a bit excessive for a four-hour drive, wouldn't you?"

Julia laughed. "C'mon. Let's get Ava inside. She'll be more comfortable here than in the car."

Even though the drive to Petoskey had been challenging, Julia was exhilarated by the sights and sounds of summer on Walloon Lake. Over the past two months, she'd been mentioning the idea to Cam, and she remembered when Cam had finally agreed…

"But she'll be so far away. What if something happens to her and I'm way down here?" Cam said.

They'd been at Connor's house during one of the drop-offs when Julia had brought it up, and she'd asked Connor ahead of time not to interfere.

"I won't let her out of our sight for a minute. I promise. We'll be just as diligent about watching her there as we are here," Julia said.

Cam appeared to be considering it, but Julia could tell she still wasn't sold. And then she remembered something. Maybe it was underhanded, but she needed to use everything in her arsenal to convince Cam.

"Didn't you say you wanted to take Ava to visit your sister in Denver this fall?"

"Well…yes…but…"

"Imagine how we'll feel when she's all the way across the country. At least Petoskey is only a few hours away," Julia said.

Connor shot her an approving look before he ducked his head back down and continued playing with Ava.

"But that's different. I'm her mother," Cam argued. And then everyone froze except for Ava, who had just knocked over a tower of blocks and was giggling.

The adults exchanged looks and waited for someone to speak. Finally, Connor, who had abided by Julia's wishes up until then, spoke up.

"I'm her father, and I'm going to miss Ava when she goes to Denver just as much as you're going to miss her when we go Up North. We both have to compromise, Cam."

That did the trick. Cam stopped arguing and agreed to let Ava go as long as they called her every day and sent pictures of Ava to assure Cam that she was fine.

"Hell, we'll Facetime with you if that'll make you feel better," Connor said. And then noticing the disgruntled expressions on Julia's and Cam's faces, he said, "What? I thought that was a good idea."

Julia shook her head. "It's a fine idea. We're upset about you swearing in front of Ava."

"She's right. Julia and I talked about this the other day. Ava's starting to learn more words, and we don't want her to pick up any of your bad ones!"

"Oh. Sorry," Connor said.

And now here they were, loaded down with luggage for a four-day stay. It would be just the three of them on Thursday and Friday, and then Julia's parents were joining them on Saturday and Sunday.

Since meeting Ava earlier in the summer, Julia's parents had made a concerted effort to smooth things over with Connor just as Julia had anticipated. They'd fallen in love with Ava at first sight, and there were no further mentions of Alec.

Connor and her father might never be the best of friends, but as long as they were respectful of each other, that was all Julia could ask for. Debra, on the other hand, had become quite enamored with Connor and, of course, with Ava. She'd offered to be a backup babysitter for them any time, and between her, Barbara, Harper, and McKayla, they had a whole slew of helpers at their disposal.

When Julia had asked her parents if she and Connor could use the lake house, they'd immediately said yes. But when she'd mentioned that they were bringing Ava too, her mom had asked if they would mind having company for a couple of days. How could Julia say no? Besides it being their house, she wanted her parents to spend more time getting to know Connor and Ava. Plus, with her parents there, she and Connor might be able to sneak in some alone time.

They were still adjusting to having Ava in their lives, but they were doing it together, and the thought of that was thrilling to her. Her life had become so full of love and happiness that she went around with a perma-smile.

Since that day in the park when she and Connor had exchanged I love yous, they'd talked about marriage in vague terms. A lot of their sentences started with "When we get married…" or "When we have more kids…" They hadn't gotten engaged yet, but she felt sure they would someday. In the meantime, Finn and Harper had recently announced their engagement at a July Fourth barbecue at Mr. and Mrs. O'Brien's house.

Nobody had been surprised, least of all Julia, who could tell the second she'd seen Harper that something was up. Harper was the worst secret keeper on the planet, and when Julia saw her hiding her left hand behind her back, she knew. She pulled Harper aside, and making sure that nobody could hear, she whispered, "Show me your hand."

"Why?" Harper said, playing dumb.

"Just show me your left hand."

That was all it took. Harper excitedly pulled out her left hand from behind her back and waved it in front of Julia, after which, they'd jumped up and down like teenagers.

"I'm so happy for you!" Julia exclaimed, and she might have said it a bit too loud because, before long, they were surrounded.

First, it had been Liam, who'd been walking by with a plate piled high with food. He'd stopped in his tracks and said, "What was that I just heard? Are you two finally engaged?"

Julia smiled, thinking that he could have been directing his question to either one of them. Everyone in the family knew how she and Connor felt about each other. But Liam zeroed in on Harper, who had snapped her left hand behind her back again.

"What's going on?" McKayla said as she came up beside them.

"Harper and Finn are engaged," Liam replied.

"Well, it's about time," McKayla said.

If Julia was sometimes loud, McKayla was even louder, and the next thing they knew, Finn, Connor, Barbara, and Daniel had gathered around them.

Finn looked at Harper quizzically, and she shrugged. "It's Julia's fault," she said.

"What is?" Barbara asked.

"I thought we were going to do this after dinner," Finn said, but his eyes were sparkling.

"Do what? What is everyone talking about?" Barbara said, growing more excitable by the moment.

"Calm down, honey. They'll tell us when they're ready," Daniel said.

Taking a deep breath, Finn said, "Mom, Dad, Harper and I are—"

"Engaged!" Liam finished, which earned him a punch on each arm from both of his brothers.

"You idiot! You were supposed to let them tell," Connor said.

"Sorry, but it's not a big surprise. They've been together forever. I'm already taking bets on when you and Julia will be getting engaged."

A few months ago, Liam's comment would have caused Julia to shrink with embarrassment, but not anymore. She just smiled brightly at Connor, who smiled back.

"See? I'm guessing two or three months, tops," Liam said, which earned him another punch from Connor.

"And you'll probably wreck their announcement too," Finn said.

After that, they all sat down to eat and to discuss Finn and Harper's wedding plans.

"We don't want anything too big," Harper said. "We want it to be simple and preferably outdoors."

"Wouldn't it be so cool if you got married on Jekyll Island at the same time as Will and Megan?" Julia said. But looking at Finn's expression, she realized her mistake.

"Uh, no," he said. "I'm not real interested in sharing my wedding day with a man Harper used to date."

Harper shook her head at him. "You could hardly call it dating. We only went out a few times, and we only kissed once."

"Didn't need to be reminded of that," Finn said, knocking back his beer.

"When are Will and Megan getting married anyway?" McKayla asked.

"They're thinking around Valentine's Day," Julia replied.

Up until then, McKayla and Liam had been kind of quiet, and Julia wondered what might be going on with them. She assumed that McKayla had been invited to the barbecue to celebrate Harper's engagement, but maybe there was another reason she was there.

"February will be the perfect time to get out of Michigan for a while," Harper said.

And then the conversation drifted off to other topics.

As Connor stumbled into the lake house with all their bags, Julia was brought back to the present.

"Do we really need all this stuff for *four* days?" he asked as he set the bags in the foyer and came into the living room to join her and Ava.

"Yes. We really do," she replied, laughing.

"What all is in there, anyway?"

"Do you really want to know?"

"Probably not," he said. "Whatever it is, I trust you."

"Here. Why don't you hold Ava while I start to unpack?" When she went to hand Ava to him, Julia said, "Go to Da-da."

"Da-da," Ava repeated.

Julia froze with Ava suspended between them.

"Did you hear that?" Connor asked.

"I think she said Da-da," Julia said.

"Da-da," Ava said.

"Oh my God. She did say it!" Connor said, taking Ava from Julia and planting kisses all over her chubby cheeks.

They'd been trying to get Ava to say Da-da for the past few weeks, and while she'd made some attempts, the words hadn't come out clearly until then.

As if she could sense how happy she'd made them, Ava said it a few more times. "Da-da, da-da, da-da." She was rewarded with more kisses from Connor and a tight squeeze from Julia.

"This is so exciting! We should probably call Cam and tell her," Julia said.

Connor shook his head. "Not yet. I want it to just be the three of us for a little while longer."

One look into his eyes and she melted, just like always. "Okay," she said softly.

The next two days were idyllic. They slathered Ava with sunscreen and sat with her at the water's edge, taking turns holding her in their laps and letting her splash in the water. Julia was put in charge of picture-taking, and she sent dozens of photos to Cam to assure her that Ava was safe and having fun.

But since it was their watch, they took a few liberties, such as letting Ava play in the sand and getting completely dirty before they rinsed her off in the lake. She'd had on a pair of baby sunglasses (princess ones of course), and Julia had been diligent about keeping the sand out of Ava's eyes. But still, she had a feeling that Cam wouldn't have approved if she'd have known.

At night, Connor grilled hamburgers and hot dogs for them, and they ate outside on the deck, with Ava in a seat that hooked onto the table.

"I would have never known about this contraption if you hadn't thought of it," Connor said, shaking his head in amazement.

She smiled and said, "See. She really does need all this stuff."

When Julia's parents arrived on Saturday, she and Connor eagerly let them take over with Ava. For the first two nights, they'd let Ava sleep in the portable crib in the room they shared, but once Debra got there, she insisted they move the crib to the master bedroom, which was much larger.

Julia had hesitated at first, wondering how Cam would feel about it, but then Connor had reminded her that her dad was a pediatrician.

"If anyone can take care of Ava, he can," Connor had said.

So, on Saturday evening, after swimming, boating, and picnicking on the lawn, Julia and Connor settled into their room—alone.

Smiling, she curled into his side and laid her hand on his bare chest.

"I love you," she whispered.

"I love you too."

He turned on his side so he could look into her eyes, which were brimming with love and contentment.

"I can't wait until we have a baby of our own," he said, "but first, I want to marry you. From here on out, no more mistakes."

Caressing his face with the back of her hand, she said, "Loving you could never be a mistake. And if it is, it's the sweetest mistake I'll ever make."

THE END

Stay tuned for Liam and McKayla's story in Book Three of the O'Brien Brothers series.

Author's Note:

If you enjoyed *The Sweetest Mistake*, please take a moment to leave a review on Amazon and/or Goodreads. And while you're there, check out my other sweet and sexy contemporary romance novels!

I love to connect with readers. Please visit my website (susancoventry.org), or follow me on Facebook, Instagram, and Twitter.

Thanks for reading!

Susan

Made in United States
Orlando, FL
27 November 2023

39383136R00153